With Love, From Japan
Stories and Essays

Steve Baba

Crimson Milk Press

San Francisco

Cover design: Steve Baba

Ways to contact the author:
www.stevebaba.com
facebook.com/stevebaba
twitter.com/stevenhbaba
withlovefromjapan@gmail.com

First printing, June 2014
Printed in the USA

ISBN: 0615986269
ISBN-13: 978-0615986265

These stories were originally published in the following magazine Daily Love;

A Night Out 2/23/2013
Her Ghost 1/15/2011
With Love, From Japan 2/22/2013
Call 2/20/2011

Table of Contents

Acknowledgements

For all my family and friends. Thanks especially to Yuri Nishimura for the inspiration to write short stories again. Also thanks to Steven Suzui, my namesake. Kudos to Jim Pacelli for believing in me. And to my forever muse, Tiffany Silverman.

For Yuri

A Night Out

I met her on the street. I met her on the playground. We were ten. No, we met on the street. It was cloudy this mild autumn evening. The street was slick with rain. She was beautiful. Wonderful almond brown eyes. A small nose. Perfect pink lips. Medium length black hair. She smiled when she saw me. We greeted each other. I asked her if she was ready to go. She nodded. We crossed the street and walked a couple of blocks. Then I realized we went the wrong way.

We turned around and she laughed. All I could do was look straight ahead. I wasn't embarrassed. I wasn't ashamed. I asked her her name. Yuri. My name is Steve. How old are you? I'm 23. I'm from Japan. I'm here to learn English. How old are you? What? I almost forgot her words. Oh, I'm 28, I lied. What do you do? I'm a poet. I write poems for a living.

We made it to the restaurant. We were admitted immediately. She took off her tan overcoat and sat down. Where were my manners? I took off my jacket and sat down. We ordered beer and sashimi. I didn't notice the waitress. Yuri looked into my eyes and I saw questions.

After the first of the beers went down our throats, a light blush was painted on her cheeks. So how is it being a poet? I like it. No, I love it. It is my calling. It is my career. And what do you do in Japan? I work in an office. It's not boring, but I wish I were doing something else. The food came and it was delicious. Sashimi with soy sauce. She took it with wasabi. I did not. We ordered some fried chicken pieces and a kind of cake that had fish in it.

I love my life. I am in love with life. I could be in love with you too. She took a piece of chicken and smoothly put it in her mouth. I watched her the whole time. I ate too. Drank some more beer. I told her my family was descended from samurai. She said her family came from peasants. You should come to Japan. She answered what I was thinking. I would love to see the cherry blossom festival. You would love it. I think I would. I then excused myself. I need to go outside to smoke. You smoke? Yes, I'm sorry. Why was I sorry? I was. I glanced at the nicotine stain on my left middle finger. I hoped she didn't see it.

She said she was from Osaka. But lived in Tokyo. She liked life in Tokyo. But missed Osaka. That's where her family was. She said her mother had just separated from her father. I would never do that to you.

More and more, I could feel her in my heart. And it wasn't because of the beer. We talked throughout the night. Then we had to go. I was downcast. I put her overcoat on her. I tied my jacket to my waist. I was too hot. Too hot. I opened the door for her and there was a light rain coming down. She opened a black umbrella, and I walked like a naked man in the dark.

I asked her if she was going to come back to San Francisco. She said she didn't know. I wanted to ask her: What if you did if it were for someone special? We walked back to the corner where we met. The children around us giggled and ran around the playground. I wish I had had a rose to give her. Instead I gave her my favorite rock. The rain came down harder, and I realized we were still standing on the sidewalk. I hugged her and said I would call her. I watched her skip down the stairs to the subway. My heart was finally pierced.

Karima

Thank you. Thank you for everything. It was great spending time with you. I had a blast. Now you are off to France and I am blue. When we walked to the subway, I kept on thinking how it would be without you. And I didn't like it. I didn't like it one bit. But this is reality. And I must accept it.

You came into my life on a warm, sunny morning in October. I saw you smoking while feeling the warmth of the sun. I sat down next to you and I felt alive. I lit my cigarette and I asked you your name. Karima. I smiled, not knowing that the next three months would change my life. We got to know each other for a little bit. You said you were from France and I asked where. Toulouse. Ah. Never been there, but I have a friend living there. You should come. You can come stay at my house. Wow. I never got an invitation so early in learning more about someone. So why are you here in San Francisco? I'm here to learn belly dancing. Interesting. I hope you enjoy your stay. Thanks Steve!

We didn't see much of each other the first few days you were here. I would see you when I came up to smoke throughout the days, and maybe at odd times when we ate at the same time. You were always smiling and cheerful. I liked your countenance. I observed that you were kind. You were always friendly to the other roommates, and you always greeted me.

The first thing you did for me was offer tobacco to me. When I ran out of cigarettes one day, you gave me a packet of tobacco. Virginia Golden. You got it duty-free from the airport in Madrid. That was really kind of you and I appreciated it very much. It was always good seeing you when we had time to talk and smoke. You told me a little more about your belly dancing classes. They were from Tuesday to Saturday and from 6 to 8:30 pm. You were always drinking coffee when we smoked in the morning.

With the days going by, and us seeing each other more often, we became good friends. We sat at the kitchen table as you looked at your computer. We ate together, though we cooked separately. We still smoked together when our schedules met. But we weren't close. Not yet. I would come to visit you in your room in the evenings to talk. I liked being around you and it was so nice to hear about your days. You taught me some phrases in French. Bonne nuit. Ca va. A bientot. We also spoke in Spanish when you didn't know how to say the words in English. It was really fun learning a new language and also speaking Spanish again.

When we talked, you told me how you loved the people of San Francisco. They were always kind to you and that they always chatted with you on the street, they hugged you, and they asked what you were doing. You had that kind of charm and friendliness. Your fellow belly dancing students were intrigued by your French, and they came to you with open arms. Even the teachers, who were the best in the world, acted like you were their child, they your mother. You liked the weather. In France, you told me that it was quite cold now. Not like here.

We had a conversation about France. You didn't like living there because there were racist undertones in the streets. Sometimes at night, police would stop you and ask you questions. People in the cafes and restaurants would purposely make you wait to ask you for your order. They were cold in the bakeries and supermarkets. I thought this was sad. This is why you liked San Francisco and America. It was so free here. And safer too. You told me that in your city, Toulouse, and even Paris, it was dangerous to go out at night. I was perplexed because from all the stories I had heard from people who had visited there and from books it was as safe, if not safer than any city in America. I was wrong, you told me. And I believed you.

Then one evening, you opened up and told me your story. You told me you weren't in San Francisco just to take belly dancing classes. You were there because of a dream. Last year, your brother died in a car accident. He was so young. It devastated the family. So each family member took a piece of paper and wrote down what they would want to do with their lives in the future. For him. Because of him. You didn't want to forget. So you wrote down that you wanted to come to San Francisco to learn from the best belly dancers. You wanted to come here because you wanted to fulfill a dream. I was crying inside because you were realizing your dream, and I knew that this was the most important thing for you.

The second thing you offered to me was food. I ran out of food one night and you asked if I had eaten. I said no. You gave me some of the food you made. It was delicious. And I was so happy that you offered it to me. You said that it is imperative, and important, that sharing food, tobacco, and money, when possible, was something someone should share if you had it. The next day you gave me some of your rice to make so I could eat. I was grateful. You didn't have to do that, but you did.

You continued your schedule of going to belly dancing classes. When you came home, I was waiting for you so we could smoke together and talk about our days. You told me that the classes were difficult, but fun. The students and teachers made all the difference.

I shared my DVDs with you. You had a lot of downtime in the late evenings. Sometimes you would watch belly dancing videos on the Internet. Other times you would watch the news about France and Toulouse. So I wondered if you would like to watch some movies instead. You happily accepted. I gave you four movies. We actually watched Before Sunset together in your room. You loved it.

One night, you were smoking outside. You heard a noise. You didn't know what it was. So you looked into the darkness and saw a shadow of a creature on the fence. It was a raccoon. You froze and you wanted to scream. But you didn't. You put out your cigarette quickly and hurriedly came into the house. You told me what you saw. I said they were harmless. You weren't too sure of that. So from now on, when you smoked in the evenings, I would have to smoke with you. Or at least keep you company.

We got closer and closer as the weeks went by. We talked, smoked, ate and enjoyed each other's company. This was a good life. And you were fulfilling a dream. You missed your family and friends, but it was good to be where you were. Here in San Francisco. I knew in my heart that I would be sad the day you left. I told you I was going to cry when you went home. You told me not to. Be happy, you said. Be happy. We celebrated your birthday the day after Thanksgiving. You were 33. This was the first birthday that you weren't with your family. It was okay, though. You had some good friends around you. You had me. We drank a little white wine and you bought some chocolate for yourself. We talked until one in the morning.

With the days getting shorter, with the time with you dwindling, I felt so awful. But I reminded myself that I should cherish these last days with you. Or I would regret it. So I cheered myself up, and met you every night for the last three weeks you were here. You said you would be sad too. But life is strange. We will meet again. Meet again.

Then it was Friday. You were leaving in four days. So I took you out to lunch. We went to this Peruvian restaurant. We both had the same dish of marinated chicken. I had a sangria, you had water. We chatted about what would happen when you went back to France. I would be here for another 6 months. You would enjoy the holidays with your family, and then back to work in January. After we finished our lunch, we had some chocolate cake. After that, we went

18

to a cafe and had some espresso. You were really happy and it was good to see you happy. My heart intermittently went from being warm and uplifted to cold and sad. I felt like a storm was coming and the rain was going to drench me from head to toe.

Saturday. You invited me and some fellow roommates to your friend's café. We went around 3 pm. The café was called Muddy Waters. It was nice with wood floors and creaky chairs. Your friend was so nice to us. She talked in Moroccan-accented English. You paid for our drinks ahead of time, so they were free for us. We sat and chatted for a couple hours. People in Santa costumes were passing the café. Yes, it was the holidays.

Finally you offered your true friendship. After all the days and weeks of talking, smoking and sharing time together, I knew that you were a true friend. You gave this to me with a full heart. I gave you my friendship as well and you were grateful for it. It was going to be hard to say goodbye tomorrow. We hung out for the last moments together, and then when it got too late, you went to bed. I didn't sleep well, and I really needed a drink.

Tuesday morning. I woke up and had one last cigarette with you. We smoked in silence. I could sense the excitement in your body language. You were going home. Home at last. We gathered your belongings and started the long walk to the BART station. When we went outside, the wind was bitterly cold. It figured. The sun was covered by grey clouds. We walked the 15 minutes to the station. Then it was the moment I had dreaded since I knew you would be going home. We stood in front of each other for a moment, without a word spoken. I didn't know what to say. But my heart told me to say something memorable. So I said, "Have a good trip home. Je t'aime mon ami." You said the same to me. We hugged for what seemed like an eternity. I saw tears in your eyes. I felt like a big weight had been put into my stomach, and it was going to pull me to the ground. You turned away and went into the station. And then you were gone. You were gone.

I walked back to the house with the wind still whipping away in my hair and clothes. I needed a drink. The sadness I felt was something I hadn't felt in a very long time. And so goodbye to you, Karima. We will meet again.

Time To Say Goodbye

As I entered the airport from the terminal, I was blasted by a hot, humid air that made me sweat instantly. My clothes clung to my body, droplets of perspiration dripped into my eyes and I was losing my grip on the over-packed suitcase in my left hand. Honolulu was always like this. It didn't matter if it were raining, clear, or winter, it would always be humid. After Hawaii had welcomed me with open arms, I looked through the crowds of people that congested the gate. Grandpa. He was always on time when he picked me up. Where was he? Damn. I forgot. He wouldn't be here today. I looked down and felt my heart drop into my stomach. I pushed my way through the sea of sweating humans, and held back the tears that were crying out to be released. I felt as if everyone were staring at me. They weren't. I made it past the human tourist parade, and made it to the walk bridge that connected this section of the airport with the rest. It was an open air bridge, and I stopped to the side to catch my breath. The high-pitched sounds of airplane engines pierced into my ears. The skies were a cobalt blue. No clouds today. I gathered my thoughts, and headed to the baggage claim. I had come many times to Hawaii before, my first time being 6 months old. All those previous trips were to see my family. My mom was from Hawaii. We always spent two to three weeks living at my grandma and grandpa's house in Palolo Valley. But this time the trip was not for vacation. It was a trip to say goodbye.

I made it unscathed to baggage claim carousel E-1. My United Airlines flight was posted on the electronic sign. The metal plates rotated around and around. The air conditioning making me shiver. Then the luggage lumbered out, one by one, all different shapes and colors. I wondered where my mom was. She was supposed to pick me up. I jockeyed my way to the front of the carousel. A choice spot where the luggage was coming right out. I stared blankly into the opening, praying my backpack made the trip without incident. A rather large woman bumped me in the back. *Sorry dear.* She had a Southern accent. I shrugged, and then she elbowed me as she reached for a canary yellow suitcase with stickers all over it. I scowled at her. She didn't see. She was too busy elbowing everyone else out of the way. I saw my red backpack expectorate out of the opening, and as I reached to grab it, someone pulled me back. I looked behind me, my face dark with anger. It was Mom. I relaxed, and gave her a hug. We didn't say anything. We were feeling the same thing. I watched my backpack do the loop, and when it came around again, I jumped forward, and with razor-sharp precision, grabbed the backpack exactly on the leather handle. I grunted and pulled the overstuffed thing onto the floor. It was time to go home.

My mom brought the Lexus. My grandma's new car. I guess Mom didn't want to drive Grandpa's Buick. That thing was always so hard to drive. I chuckled as we walked into the parking garage. I remembered the time I was learning to drive that grey boat, and when I was parallel parking it into a microscopic parking space, I managed to hook the rear bumper under the adjacent van behind. I never drove that car again.

The drive home was always ceremonial. It was the re-acquaintance of my adopted home. The view from the H-1 freeway could be a tourist attraction in itself. First, you could see Pearl Harbor from the south, with its battleships and Navy personnel. Then the dazzling blue water reflecting the noonday sun. In the north, Manoa Valley was always lush and green. I have never seen it brown in all my years I had visited. There was the Hawaii Rainbow Warrior stadium at the base of the valley. And then our exit at 6th Avenue. We didn't say a word to each other as the car went up the exit ramp except for my mom asking me how the flight was. I knew we would be talking a lot more when we reached the house.

We drove up to the garage and I felt a little better. Grandma and Grandpa's house was like a refuge. The house had been there for over 40 years and it still held up after all the rain that usually came to the valley in the early afternoons. I opened the car door and got my luggage from the trunk. We walked up the unruly stairs from the garage to the inner part of the house. I glanced at the pikake tree near the garage and it was in full bloom. I took off my shoes as was customary for our family, and put my luggage down.

I walked into the big kitchen and saw it was still the same blue and white that I had seen for many a time. Nothing was cooking, however. I went to the living room where my grandma's bed was. She was sitting up and

23

watching the news. Grandma was a news junkie just like me. She saw me and smiled. I kissed her on the cheek and hugged her tightly. She once told me she wouldn't hug me anymore because I hugged her too tightly. But this time it was different. I saw my sisters Andrea and Erin sitting in chairs near the television. My dad would be coming tomorrow. I sighed and sat down. Grandma asked if I was hungry, and I said a little. She offered some kakimochi and I ate some. Ah, that familiar taste of rice and soy sauce. Couldn't get that in San Jose.

We didn't do much that first day I was in Hawaii. We just enjoyed each other's company and all of us held our grief inside. I was doing okay. I knew when I saw his body, some emotions would come out. But that was a ways away. I went to bed early and had a good, dreamless sleep.

My dad was at the house by noon. My mom did the same thing with me and picked him up at the airport. He was somber when he came into the house. He hadn't been to Hawaii for many years. Work or sports always called to him when we went in the summers. This was June, so it would be a busy time for him. But he loved my grandpa dearly and was making an exception. We sat around doing nothing. I felt like I wanted to talk about it, but it didn't feel like the right time. So we just ate, drank (no alcohol), and rested.

Today was going to be hard. I would be seeing my grandpa for the very last time. We got up early and had a breakfast of eggs and bacon. The air filled with the odor of good food. It reminded me of Sundays when my grandpa would cook breakfast for me, my grandma, and himself. He was always happy cooking. I looked at the chopstick drawer and looked longingly at his pair. We went off to the funeral home. Two cars. Yes, our family was that big now. We went into the lobby, and the funeral director said it would be a few minutes. I sat and stared at the wall, not knowing what would happen next. I asked offhandedly what the will said. My dad said that everything was being bequeathed to my grandma. And as it should be, I thought to myself.

We were ushered into the viewing room. The first thing that I saw was the open lid of a coffin. It was plush in the interior and impersonal on the outside. Then his body. He looked like he was at peace. The cancer that had ravaged him did not win. He went out on his own terms. He was wearing his favorite Hawaiian dress shirt and a pair of tan slacks. His eyelids seemed strange, though. They looked like they were half-open. But I couldn't see the cold reality of death in them. We stood there looking for a few minutes, then went outside to go back home. I didn't feel anything until we exited the funeral home. I put on my sunglasses, and then a wave of grief hit me like a giant-sized boulder. I sobbed for a second, then held myself together. Erin asked if I was okay, and I nodded solemnly. The last thing I remember is one of the workers at the funeral home smoking a cigarette.

The funeral was to be held on Saturday. That was a couple days away. We didn't do anything. We didn't go to the beach. We didn't go to the mall. We ate in. My dad and

I had a beer and sat on the porch in silence. I missed the barbeques my grandpa used to have when all of the family was here in the summer. We usually came in August every year. He would cook steaks as thick as my hands, and also make baked potatoes and salad. The thick cloud of sadness seemed to dissipate from the house.

Saturday came. And it was time to really say goodbye. I wasn't slated to read at the funeral, but wished I had had a poem to read. In later years I would write about my grandpa explicitly. It made me feel good, and the memories were like a newspaper, with each experience with him in each article. We all dressed up. I wore a nice Hawaiian shirt and a pair of black pants. My sisters were in dark-colored dresses and my parents dressed in black. My grandma refused to wear a dress. She wore her jeans and a nice colorful blouse. We went to the church early in the day, as we wanted to inspect the places where we would have the memorial as well as where the people sat and where the food would be. It all looked good, and we took our seats and waited.

People came in earlier than expected. It wasn't surprising, since my grandpa was well loved in Hawaii. Extended family members came in droves. Friends, co-workers and acquaintances came. I remember one man who was so filled with sadness, that when he shook each of our hands, he had to take his handkerchief and wipe away free-flowing tears. Then it started. Everyone stared at the cremated remains of my grandpa every minute. I felt at peace and was happy that grandpa was in heaven now.

The memorial was poignant and full of positive thoughts. When my cousin Eddie-Boy read his eulogy, I almost cried. But I had to be strong. His voice cracked when he came to a particularly moving passage. I looked at Grandma and she was weeping. Everyone in the church was crying. But I held up. I don't know why, but I felt I had to be strong. So I was.

When the memorial was over, we ate. There was so much food, I don't know what we did with the leftovers later. But everyone was able to have a full stomach. It was good. We talked and had a nice time seeing relatives that I hadn't seen in years. Auntie Jane was my favorite aunt and she always had a smile on her face. But the loss of Grandpa was too much for her. I sat next to her eating my food and I smelled her familiar perfume in the air. She put her arm around my shoulders and said I was a good boy. Grandpa would surely miss you.

My nephew was born almost one month to the day before my grandpa died. He was a little thing, so cute. His first trip to Hawaii and he was only one month old! He was a little restless, but calmed down. But after the memorial, he was really agitated. My sister held him over her shoulder and he cried and cried. Maybe he felt what all of us felt. My mom said that maybe Darrien was like a sign. Take something away, and receive something. I think my grandpa would have loved Darrien. He would have been the third male in the family, with me being first, and my cousin Ryan being the second. Yeah, Grandpa would have been proud of my sister and our family.

We drove home and I felt a glow that I hadn't felt in a very long time. We went into the house and started the evening drinking. Just like him. He always had a beer or few after work. It was time to remember.

There was a time when we were at the beach house and he was drunk. He caught a couple of stick fish with that old, antiquated hand-held fishing net. The times he let my sisters and I take advantage of him. Two memories are still in my mind about that. The first was when my sister Andrea and I took a blue ball point pen and drew tattoos on his chest and arms. I think we made a ship on his chest and at least one anchor on his arm. The other time was when we tied my grandpa up in a chair on Christmas morning when I was ten. He just took it all in stride and let us be kids.

Grandpa loved autumn. He and my grandma would come to San Jose to see the leaves change color and feel the cool air. We would all be in school and Grandpa would walk us there in the mornings. Sometimes he would carry my sister on his shoulders while he held my hand. One time he gave lunch money to a child who didn't have any.

I went to bed happy and fresh. My family felt whole again. That night, I dreamt of my grandpa. We were in his huge, gray Buick and we were driving on the highway to the western side of the island. Sometimes the rain came, but only in spurts. The easy listening music was playing on the radio, and he asked me when I would be ready to drive. We reached the west side in twenty minutes. Soon we would see kids coming and going to the beach. Many small Mom and Pop stores were scattered alongside the highway. We finally reached Waianae. The sun was coming out intermittently and we parked next to the beach we would come to and had come to for years. I unpacked my surfing gear and he would get the cooler with Schlitz malt beer and the Sunday paper. I went into the water and he would read his paper while sipping beer. He offered a can to a man who was shading himself under a palm tree. That was Grandpa. Always generous.

After surfing for a few hours, we headed to the furthest part of the island on the west. There we sat on the sand with our chairs and watched the sunset. After that, we drove back to town, and we went to Black Angus and had a couple steaks. Finally home to Grandma and the dog. I woke up and smiled.

A Trip To The Desert

Tuesday Morning, December 30, 1997

4.00a

It is still dark, as we load up the truck to head on yet another adventure. This is our third foray into new frontiers, Yosemite being the first and King's Canyon being the second. The air is thick with humidity and the night sky is covered with grey clouds. Inside I feel a shiver of excitement as the new journey begins. The truck is loaded, and with a sharp slam of my door, I strap on my seatbelt and stare out into the darkness. The thunderous start of the engine cracks through the quiet silence of a city still asleep, and the wheels rotate against the black asphalt. We are on our way south....

4.15a

We finally get to 85 South, and now it's a quick and quiet drive to hook up with 101. There are maybe three, four cars on the road to keep us company. The rhythmic bumps on the road, the yellow reflectors that divide the lanes, and the lighted exit signs are the only other companions with us. Lance loads a tape into the stereo, and some rock tunes reverberate throughout the cab. As I stare out into the darkness, I feel my eyes growing heavy with the sleep I was deprived of the night before, and I try to keep busy by making small talk with Lance. He is receptive, and it keeps us both going. An hour later we take the left turn off to 152 East, heading towards my second home away from home, Yosemite. But we won't be heading there this time....

6.24a

The light starts to creep above the mountains in the east, and the faint glow is a welcome sight from the darkness. There are a few more vehicles on the road now, and the landscape seems to be more visible. We are still heading south, but on Highway 5 now. The land that we pass by is very flat, with deep green pastures and an occasional hill. A light mist hangs low to the ground, and I can make out a few cows grazing. The sun starts to hover just over the horizon, and it looks as if heaven has touched the roof of the earth for that one poignant moment. Then the full light of the sun reflects off of the ozone, and the day has started again. We're still headed south, and now my eyes are adjusting to my new surroundings....

8.00a

The landscape hasn't changed much, so I've started to think about things. Work has been quite good, though I know that I hope to leave soon. Unfortunately that really isn't an option. I just want to go and fly like a bird, and it is times like this trip where I can at least spread my wings and do a few fly-bys outside of the cage. She is always in my mind when I start to think. I miss her. I put my hand against the window, and it is freezing. I glance at Lance, and he looks like he is deep in thought. There is something hypnotic about driving on the road. Thoughts you have forgotten, you remember. Special memories that are reflected upon. Emotions that have been hidden deep down inside of you come out. Ah, the road of life....

12.00p

We cross eastward, and are now headed to The Manzanar. A place of history and infamy, this is a sidebar journey on top of the main event. I had relatives who were there and a few of the other internment camps. I am not sure how I am going to react when we get there. I just don't know. The road runs through a dry, desolate valley, neglect of life, except for the occasional tumbleweed or man-made dirt path. Mountains rise high above us west and east. The western mountains, black and jagged, are covered with snow. The eastern mountains look like giant piles of dirt, with flat tops, as if someone had run their hand across them. The road curves, and there on the right, is a deep dry lake. Wisps of salt lie on its surface, and patches of green algae float in what is left of the water. I can faintly see the reflection of the eastern mountains in its waters. Signs for The Manzanar Internment Camp are showing up in frequency, and I know that my ancestor's past and my own present are going to meld soon....

12.30p

Lance pulls the truck up to the ancient, brown guard gate. There is a bronze plaque that tells the reader what this place was, and what it meant in American history. A billboard with even more history and a layout of The Manzanar are on the opposite side. The sky is a brilliant blue, the air a crisp cool that tastes fresh. And then it happens. My eyes start to well with tears, and I can feel my heart ache. This is it. I have never come to terms with my heritage as a Japanese-American, and at that precise moment, it hits me. I am Japanese. I am American. How would I have felt if my country disowned me, when I loved it so dearly? To be put in a desolate area, and scorned by my fellow countrymen as a traitor? I know now how they felt, as I see this place in history. We drive into the campsite, and follow the sandy path that leads to the various houses, if you can call them houses. They are now more like plots of land. Old rusty pipes sticking out of the worn-down concrete foundations are all that are left. A few buildings remain, but they are so dilapidated that it seems that just a touch would make them disintegrate. There are some dead, dry trees that are scattered throughout the camp, but not nearly enough for any type of privacy. And then the highlight of the camp- the graveyard. It is visible from afar. A giant white beacon with Japanese characters is the marker. Fenced in with crude barbwire and rotting wood, here is where some never left this place. A few tombstones lie inside, but mostly just markers. Almost all are adorned with money, letters, even toys. Rocks are laid at the base of the beacon, and I suddenly feel ashamed that I can't read the beacon. I feel a soothing, lonely peace. A cold breeze blows through, but that is all I can hear....

1.00p

We make our departure with history and I feel as if I have changed forever....We drive on and find our road that is to lead us to our final destination.

1.06p

The sun is shining brightly outside and I can feel my body temperature rising. I roll down the window and feel the lukewarm air whip through my hair and sweep across my face. The warmth from the sun feels good. We have crossed into the mountains and are descending a snake-curved road that goes all the way to the bottom of the Panamint Valley. A semi-desert, it is vast between the mountain ranges and desolate. But this would be no comparison to the place that lay ahead. Dust, dirt and rock dominate the valley floor, as we arrive at the bottom of the valley. The black asphalt looks as if a giant had smashed it to a thousand pieces, and then glued it all back together. The desert can be a very harsh environment indeed.

2.00p

We are almost there. The road rises into the mountains again and now we are skirting the tree line. Windy, weavy and unpredictable. There hasn't been a sign for miles now and now I really feel that I have left civilization. No cars. No airplanes. Just the road that has led the way from the start. We are again dropping down and now there is a sign up ahead. It says Stovepipe Springs Up Ahead. I can start to feel the adrenaline course through my veins and the weariness fades away like a memory. The truck even feels like it has picked up an unnatural speed. Then we finally see the first buildings in a hundred miles. A ranger station, a gas station, a visitor's center and many tourists and cars. As we roll into this modern oasis, there is a sign that says: Welcome to Death Valley.

Elevation 0.

2.30p

We fill up with gas and buy some literature at Stovepipe, and decide that we are going to head to Scotty's Castle. And the drive there is spectacular. We drive out of the parking lot at the ranger station and I look across the dashboard. I see these golden sand dunes that stand by themselves, peaky mountains, and a glow from the light of the sun. Majestic and mysterious. I imagine that this is what a bit of the Sahara would look like. The road follows into the valley and the Devil's Cornfield lies ahead. Giant bushes that look like giant stalks of corn grow out of the scorched, hard ground, as if a freak of nature had happened. The road follows the eastern side of Death Valley, and we are treated with a landscape that is eclectic and harsh. Colors of white, green, and gold intermix with each other. Various rock outcroppings jut out from the ground. The mountains are stained red and black, as if a massive fire had permanently scarred them. Zigzag curves contour the mountains, and it looks as if we truly are in Hell.

2.45p

We arrive at Scotty's Castle. It is a small oasis in the middle of nowhere, a haven from the harsh environments of sun and sand. In history, it was an outpost for a wealthy Englishman who was searching for gold. Castle-like structures, built in Spanish architecture, stand in defiance of the encroaching desert. Rambling around the complex, I find that this place feels like a long lost ghost town that has faded into memory. I climb the bell tower and look over what seems to be an endless tundra of sand and dirt, with the devilish mountains enclosing it. It is quite disparaging....

3.30p

The time here in the desert seems to go a lot faster than I had expected, and we only have time for one more attraction on the northern part of Death Valley; the Ubehebe Crater. The roads seem to be deteriorating the longer we drive into the desolation, and with good cause, as the ever erasing skills of the sand can make even the toughest of materials disintegrate under its unforgiving touch. A light, lukewarm breeze has made its way into the air and I can feel my eyelids starting to droop. The truck soothes its way on the desert road, and as we arrive at our next destination, we pass an ancient orange snowplow, but instead of clearing snow, it is clearing sand....

4.02p

Ubehebe Crater. It is quite a sight; not too impressive, but nonetheless an eyeful. A deep crevassing crater that sinks into the earth 360 feet, it looks like a picture of a crater on the moon. The contours that spiral downward into the crater start from a light brown on the crest, to a deep chocolate brown near the bottom. Slight wisps of sand dance briefly in the air, and the silence is complete. We stay and observe the half-mile circumference and the steep slopes for a while. The sun starts to disappear from the crater's mouth, and it is time to reach our final stop today.

4.36p

The truck slowly crawls to a stop into Furnace Creek, the place we are staying the evening. It is the main location and park headquarters of Death Valley, and a welcome sight after the long grueling day of driving. The sun lies lazily over the top of the mountains, and there are just a few minutes before sunset. We park the car on a vacant camping lot, and just sit for a moment. There are a few others that have set up camp tonight, mostly RVs. The camping lots themselves are not much to look at, with a picnic table, a small fire ring, and patches of tumbleweed accompanying the hard, sandy ground. We opt to sleep in the camper shell, as the forecast for the night is to be in the low 30's. Lance wants to set up camp quickly and then head off to the headquarters for a look-see. Camp is up in ten minutes, and we ramble off to ranger headquarters.

4.45p

Lance goes in, and I opt to stay outside and have a private moment to myself in this desert of dreams. It is serenely quiet, except for the occasional car passing by on the nearby highway. The air smells fresh and dry, even tastes good. I open my notebook and start to scribble notes about the scenery. Hard, rock-tough earth holds my feet. Various tumbleweeds and lanky bushes are scattered about. The hills to the east are the same scalded formations I saw earlier, and on the distant west the snowcapped peaks that hide the Central Valley. I feel at complete peace during this moment in time, and I reflect on the rumors I have heard about the 'cleansing' powers of the desert. I believe they are working. I see Lance exit the headquarters, and we walk back to the campsite.

5:00p

Dinnertime. Lance whips up his classic cup-o-noodles, chicken flavor. The skies start to darken, and the flames on the stove glow a hearty red. As Lance scoops the steaming noodles and broth into two plastic bowls, I watch what will be the only sunset I have ever seen in a desert. The sun has already disappeared behind the Sierra Nevada Mountains, and all that are left are the fledgling rays of light that are trying to hold on to the last bit of blue sky. The light reflects off of the streaming clouds and the colors of red, pink, orange, and purple mix together in a whirlwind of beauty. While this easel of God's hope paints the sky, the fading light reveals the blinking stars from space. Faintly at first, and then more prominent over time as the darkness takes over the light. I feel a deep ache in my heart at such a sight of perfection and a warm feeling in my boots. While mesmerized by the sunset above, I must have stepped into the fire. My boots slightly cooking, I jump out hastily and watch the rest of this divine spectacle of the desert. I miss her, and realize this is another of many other things I will want to share with her when I see her again. The light finally fades away, and the only light that keeps us company now is the campfire and my glowing boots.

7.00p

After a fitful meal of noodles and a soda or two, Lance and I talk about the day's events. We go on and on about the desert's beauty and its polarized elements. The flames of the fire seem to leap out every time we get excited about something we saw or remembered, as if the spirit of the desert was with us always. After that, a small conversation on world events and our ideas on a better world. The only sound beside our voices and the crackle of wood is a distant howl far away somewhere. Must be the wolves that inhabit the area. Time for them to hunt. Lance gets ready for bed, and he opens the camper. A quick run to the bathroom, and then Lance hops into the camper to sleep. I decide to stay up a little longer to write more about the day's travels. I make a coffee and begin to write. The air has gotten quite cold and I can see my breath between paragraphs and sips of coffee. A few minutes more and I find myself nodding incessantly. Time for bed....

Wednesday December 31, 1997 New Year's Eve

6.00a

After a deep and well-deserved sleep in the camper shell
that was as cold as an icebox, I am awakened by a loud
beep directly shrieking into my left ear. I slightly jump in
my down sleeping bag, and realize it is coming from my
watch. The first thing I see is the thick mist that emanates
from my mouth. Lance is snoring peacefully next to me,
and as I lift my head to look around the camper, I can see
that the windows are quite clouded from the moisture of
our breaths. Reaching to turn off my alarm, I perk my ears
and listen. Dead silence. Not a voice, not a sound. I put my
head down, and close my eyes. BEEP! BEEP! BEEP!
BEEP! Lance's alarm goes off at 6:35.

7.20a

Breakfast. The sky is a gloomy grey, and the absence of
sound is thick in the air. All is still, and it feels as if time
has stopped altogether. I sit on the bench and start to
scribble down some notes. Lance prepares a breakfast of
pancakes and eggs, and the whiffs of morning coffee are
addictive. As soon as breakfast is done, it is a quick pack-
up and an even quicker exit from our temporary habitat.

8.33a

We drive less than a mile to reach this long forgotten
mine that has been a cornerstone to Death Valley's history.
Back in the late 1800's, borax was mined from the valley
floor, and now stands an exhibit to signify it. As we walk

up to the exhibit, the land seems coated in snow, yet the white substance that dusts the ground is hard and glued to the surface. Borax. A couple of historic billboards on the borax mines and their miners, an authentic red water wagon, and the borax mine itself adorn the landmark area. The air is still as I read the history notes and study the gigantic water wagon that could quench the thirst of over 50 men. I could well imagine how hot it must have been under the ground, with the scorching and unforgiving sun lending its heat to the thin air within those cavernous and lonely passages. There is a man-made road that leads into the borax area, and we decide to take a small tour of the borax itself. The ground is quite rough, as the truck takes in many shocks and bumps into the borax-covered earth. The road leads into a small canyon, and as we go between these two twenty-foot high walls of borax, it seems like we have gone to another planet; Mars or even the moon maybe. We drive out the other end, and it leads back to the main highway.

8.45a

We are off to the southeast part of the park, and are going to see two major attractions along the way; Artist's Palette and Badwater. The road is a long, windy affair with such curves and dips that it feels like a roller coaster of sorts. The first stop on the list is Artist's Palette. You can even see it from the road. It is a slice of hills that are contoured with different colors, ranging from a pastel green on the tops of the hills, to rouge red on the bottoms. A small, curved-like road dices through the hills like a tour, and as we drive right up to Artist's Palette, the colors are even more eclectic to see. We take some pictures and walk along the rocky hills to get different perspectives of Artist's Palette, and then it is another quick exit.

9.33a

Alas, I have forgotten one of the true highlights of the trip; The Devil's Golf Course. A dirt road connects with the highway and it leads all the way in what seems in the middle of Death Valley. We look out over what is called The Devil's Golf Course, and the name fits the geography. It looks like a golf course, with divots and holes all over the landscape, covered again by the ever-present borax. Teeing off at 9:35, Steve and Lance. With Satan himself no less. I wonder who would have won…. As I had observed our current position at The Golf Course, I realize that everywhere we go it is deathly quiet. Too quiet. Not a bird is chirping, not a car is honking. Just Silent. The grey sky hangs in the air like a damned soul, resigned to his or her fate of living in Hell. It is quite an eerie feeling, and one I hope I never feel again. A word springs to mind- Empty.

10.00a

The geographical lowest point in the Western Hemisphere, and second lowest point on the entire planet, Badwater sounds like one of those old cowboy towns in the West. Cliffs stand over the parking lots and bathroom, and a trail leads out to an official benchmark. But we don't even get past the sign that stands in a patch of stagnant and residual water that reads: Badwater-Elevation- 232 Feet

Below Sea Level. Up on the cliffs above, there is another sign that reads: Sea Level. We have seen enough of the surface of the park and valley, so it is time to go up. Way up....

10.20a

We are headed up into the mountains on the eastern side of Death Valley, and as always, the road is there to show the way. The skies start to clear a bit, keeping the ever enclosing grey at bay, and the sun shines semi-warm through the windshield. Weaving there, winding here, dropping and rising everywhere. Though a well-paved road, it is very much unpredictable. The landscape is harsh; empty dirt valleys, an occasional sign to signify human existence in the area, and a lone car or two that passes by are all that is there to see. We start to actually climb up into the mountains, and it is very steep indeed. Up, up we go, climbing feet at exponential rates. As we finally level out, we have reached the top of our next destination, Dante's View.

11.25a

Dante's View. The single greatest point to see Death Valley in all its sprawling glory. The vastness of the valley is defined greatly here. It seems the long arm of the desert reaches forever north to south. White and red, with the minerals swirling on the surface of the valley, it looks like a sea of salt. The air bites at the flesh and a freezing wind chills bones. A short hike to a hiking path, and the drop off to oblivion, or the elevator to Hell. I have seen many beautiful natural things in the world, but nothing has had such a strange beauty as Death Valley. We spend half an hour overlooking this place of Death and Life, and then it is time for our final departure.

12.22p

We race down the mountain and back into the valley, following the road southward on the east side of the park. Rough, and a bit rocky, the road looks like it had gone through some harsh weather conditions. As we leave the park, we go around these great piles of rock and dirt called alluvial fans. They are gigantic; at least a half mile in circumference, and at least thirty feet high, maybe higher. The signs are telling us that the exit to the park is near, and as I sit there and think of what I have observed and have seen, I know that this place, though strange and desolate, has captured my soul. Never have I seen such a place full of opposites. The desert is truly a romantic place...

Epilogue-Afternoon December 31, 1997/New Year's Day 1998

We speed to Baker, California for gas, and then a quick jaunt to Highway 5, all the way back towards Salinas, where we are to spend New Year's Eve with Lance's brother and his wife. I have been overcome most of the drive back, mostly because it seems we disappeared from the face of the earth, and miraculously reappeared into civilization in the form of a city of 6,000,000 people (Los Angeles), gas stations, and Frito-Lay corn chips. Death Valley is truly the end of the earth, or more succinctly, Hell on Earth. It will be a long time before I go back again, and next time I want to be there when the temperature matches the scenery....

Squeek's Escape

The first thing I see is light. It is a bright thing, the light. Very white, if I would know of colors, and very encompassing. I see a tree; a stickly thin-branched tree that is reaching out at all angles. Sometimes I see it sway its branches back and forth with some sort of invisible force. Bushes. There are bushes. Yellowed on the tops, greener on the middles and bottoms. Cut rectangular and they stretch out for a great distance. There is a wooden fence; it looks old and well beyond its age as the brown wood is faded and tattered. There are even a couple of new, fresh boards that have replaced the ones that perhaps have fallen or rotted away. And then there is the pool. A bean-shaped aqua water colored thing that those humans go and have fun splashing and diving. It is rimmed with brick, and the patio surrounding it is made of little pebbles that seem to be all glued together. As I look outside from inside the house, I wonder what it would be like to go and feel the pebbles on my little pads, or to feel that invisible force that makes the branches on the tree move so elegantly like a dancer. And those little flying thingies. I have never seen them anywhere else before. But I can hear them chirp-chirping away, flying in the air, moving quickly. I can't take my eyes off of them. I sigh and turn away from the dirt-stained glass door that I always stare out of every day, wondering if I will ever be able to go. Dart gets to go, that old man. He goes whenever he likes, and if the human is around to open the door. He goes when it's light, he goes when it's dark. And all I can do is watch him go. Go to the freedom I so wish to have.

My fellow friends include Dart, the 18-year-old tormentor of my youth. A blue-eyed creature with a yellowish coat that has dark brown areas around his eyes and on his paws. Then there are the kids. Dizzy and Oz. They're five and six months respectively. But they don't show me any respect, as they always think my tail is a plaything and at least twenty times a day one or both of them are clawing at it or biting it. I give them a quick swipe to the head, if they pass into my comfort zone. But most of the time I try to get out of the way, running to my human's room. I'm not a fighter; I'm more of a thinker. But those two are a nuisance. I wonder if I dislike them or not. Anyway, Dizzy is a Bengal with tiger-like stripes on the front of his coat, and has leopard-like spots on his hind. He's a real feisty one and I really get mad with him when he walks by and swipes at me with his paw. What an arrogant little shit. And Oz. Oz isn't as bright as Dizzy, but he always seems to get away with everything. He has green-crossed eyes and has alternating dark orange and light orange stripes running the length of his body. I can see little blood vessels in his transparent, fleshy ears. And he always seems to be trying to start fights with Dizzy. The human likes him a lot, but I don't.

The human. What can I say about him? He feeds me, he talks to me. He is okay I guess. Pretty much my provider. But I don't like to be touched, so when he tries to pet me I shirk away. So I pretty much just go my own way, take my own space away from the others. I do feel lonely, but at the same time I can do what I want to. I can think, sleep, and relax. But those damn little shits always keep at me with their playing and running around and trying to get me to play. For a five-year-old Persian, I feel much older than that.

As I sat on top of the tower today, I looked at the mirrored wall. My green-blue eyes looked sad. My long sandy hair around my face looked saggy, my ears bent down. I attempted to lick my paws, but I didn't have the energy to clean them. Oz and Dizzy were playing down at the bottom, wrestling and biting at each other's heads. Usually Oz will cry and run away as Dizzy is the larger of the two. Dart is lying on the carpet, trying to sleep. Sometimes he'll get pissed off and go after one of the little ones if they make too much clamor. I jump down the tower and stare outside. It looks like a wonderful day. There are no clouds or rain. Just beautiful, clear light. I can hear the flying thingies chirping somewhere, most likely in the tree. Dart gets up and starts walking towards the door. I quickly run under the coffee table. The human opens the door and Dart walks out. I can feel that invisible force blow through the opening of the door and it hits me in the face. It smells so sweet and warm. I close my eyes for a second. Then I hear the door shut and the force is gone. I feel a sharp pain in my tail and I see Oz with his left paw on it, claws exposed. I screech and swipe at him. He dances away. I stare at him for a few moments, and then scamper away to the door and stare outside. I wonder if I will ever escape.

Big Sur

The car buzzed down the swervy highway on the edge of a cliff, which led down to a steep drop into the ocean. For every curve we came to, my grip on my door handle tightened. It wasn't so much that the car felt like it was going a hundred miles an hour, and that at every curve it seemed like we were going to launch off like The Dukes of Hazzard, but that at each curve there wasn't a guardrail. Jim, my faithful travel companion, thought it was the Indianapolis 500, and he tested the car's abilities, not to mention my sanity, with each twist and turn of the road. The ocean was far away and near at the same time. When I wasn't backseat driving, I would look out into the deep blue and wonder what it would be like to actually fly over the ocean; not on an airplane, but myself. I would glide up and down, marveling at the unique views I would get from my flight. And to fly forever too. Then I would hear the tires squeal around another hairpin turn, and it was back to reality. It was a bit of a drive from San Jose to Big Sur on Highway 1; the only sights were mountains or ocean. It was a pleasant, peaceful drive when we weren't skimming the edge of the asphalt. We drove across a few bridges, saw a secluded cove and encountered a river mouth where salt and fresh water melded together. As luck would have it, we were lost. Our final destination was Lime Kiln State Park, and all we knew about it was how far it was from Big Sur, which was about 22 miles south of it. We stopped at a small gas station/roadside deli, and from the words of the proprietor, she said we were to follow the road that we had been on. Jim bought a sandwich, and as we drove down the narrow, twisty highway, he proceeded to eat and drive at the same time. We were sure to fly off the road this time.

The elevations climbed and dropped, but the ocean and sun were always there. When I rolled down the window, a wonderful light wind that smelled like salt came into the car. We finally made it to our destination, with the help of the directions we got at the deli, and as we pulled into Lime Kiln State Park, I shouted with glee, as there was not only a beachside campground area, but also a forested campground area. We stopped at the camp kiosk, and a kindly old woman opened the sliding glass window. We paid for a night, and she gave us some material on the history of the park and surrounding areas. Jim put the camp sticker on the dashboard and we pulled into the beach campgrounds. Only one campground out of ten was being used, and the ground was quite gravelly and rocky. So we followed the road which led into the forest and we weren't disappointed. Thirty-two campsites, and nobody around. Nobody. We chose the last campsite; number thirty-two. It was on a high bit of ground with a running stream about twelve feet below. An old log bridge connected to the other bank, and there was a new wooden bridge just twenty paces from us. A picnic table and fire ring completed the campsite. But the main attraction was what had been standing here for many, countless years; the redwood trees that stood tall and sheltered the campsites from light. The absence of light made the area sublime and quiet. It was a bit chilly, but tranquil. It felt good to be here. We had the best of both worlds- forest and ocean. I was very happy. Jim, who was as happy as a bear in a trout-filled stream, yawned like a bear and smiled. He nodded as if he had read my mind. We unpacked the food, cooking supplies and sleeping gear. The tent went up in ten minutes.

Then our obsession started. Partington Cove. I had read about it briefly on the Internet, and I was enthralled by the natural beauty and seclusion of such a place. That was our goal for the day, to find Partington Cove. We drove out of the forest and stopped back at the kiosk. The kiosk doubled as a general store, and we both entered the small place that was sparsely stocked with maps, film, cooking supplies, and a display copy of a cord of wood. The old woman was there, and she smiled warmly when she saw us. Haven't seen anyone in days, except my crotchety husband and that fine-looking ranger man, she said. I chuckled and asked where we could find Partington Cove. She shook her head, and told us to step outside. Ray had just pulled up and he was the ranger for the day. A tall, thin man with a bushy mustache got out of the Range Rover and waved at us. We opened the door and walked out. We fielded our question to him, and he gave us brief, yet uninspiring directions to the Cove. We nodded and went back inside to buy a couple of cords of wood. Then it was a quick exit and up towards the highway in search of Partington Cove.

We drove the whole 22 miles back to Big Sur empty-handed. We followed the directions to the exact word, but to no avail. We didn't see the sign we were told of, nor were there any trails visible from the first bridge we were supposed to cross. I was a little lost for words and bit irritated. Jim, ever the optimistic one, decided to go back to the gas station and ask. A short, goateed teenager who smelled of Camels strode out and smiled. We were only the second car to fill up today. As he loaded the car up with unleaded, I asked him about Partington Cove. He told me it was on private land, but it was six miles down south. He even whipped out a map that had it marked in visible, bold letters. I thanked him, and as Jim paid the 23 dollars for the gas, I stopped and thought a bit. Pfeiffer State Beach, which was just around the corner, may be a better destination since going on private land wasn't my thing. Jim hastily agreed and we sped off. The road was a long, narrow affair that was densely covered in trees. It was a smooth road though, and it took five minutes to reach Pfeiffer. The first thing I noticed when we got out of the car was that it was quiet; no cars in the parking lot, no sounds. Just silence. A peaceful feeling. I put on my backpack and we followed the trail that was to lead us to the beach. As soon as we walked a hundred feet or so, I caught the scent of fresh salt. I knew we were there when out of the groves of trees, the sand suddenly appeared beneath our feet, and the crashing waves welcomed our eyes. It seemed a little brighter here, and the scenes of mountain to my left and stone statues of rock firmly planted in the water to my right made for a great picture. The water was a phosphorescent blue; the grey and black chunks of twenty-foot rocks rose out of the sea like giants. We decided to scramble on the rocks at the base of the mountain. The waves were crashing violently as five-foot swells spanked the naked rocks with fury. We stayed closer to the mountain, and we stood for a second at our heightened view. It was beautiful; a hidden paradise right on the ocean. I looked up the side of the mountain; its loose sandstone and steep faces were not a welcome sight. There were rough, rugged bushes scattered here and there. I sighed, hoping to find somewhere to jaunt up, but no chance. We walked further a bit, and something caught my eye. A remnant of a worn but thin path that led upwards. It was time to climb.

The first thing I ever learned about climbing was that you shouldn't carry more than you can. Obviously I never listened to that advice as I hopped from one small rock to the next, feeling the dirt beneath my feet beginning to slip away. But it seemed that right when I thought it was my time to end up on the bottom, I would make it to the next rock, or the next flat spot of the mountainside. Poor Jim got stuck following my lead, and I was hoping that a loose rock wouldn't brain him. We made it up to the twenty-foot mark, and there was a semi-big boulder that was flat and big enough for two. We stopped for some water and a look. The shadow of the mountain was fading away as the sun started to move across its path. The view was nice enough, as we could see down the beach. It was a long stretch of sand that went about a mile and a half. Then it ended into some rock. There was a curve, and on the other side was a natural rock arch. I decided to take off the backpack and strap on my fanny pack. A couple rolls of film, my camera, and we were off to the next fifty feet.

Watch out! A thirty-pound piece of mountain rolled from my left foot, and it started to plummet down the mountain. My body froze in terror as the missile aimed itself downward. I looked and saw Jim below me. His face was white and he was clinging for dear life on a bit of jutted stone. The bowling ball missed him by a foot. I gasped and let out a giant sigh. Jim looked up at me with a frown and I shook my head. We made it to the top and the scenery changed. The top was covered in prickly, dense bushes. A trail led us to the peak. The bushes disappeared and the sandstone reappeared. I wiped the sweat off my forehead and stripped down to my t-shirt. The sun felt good on my face and the slight breeze tickled my hair. The sky seemed to be right on top of us; the ocean just at the front doorstep. We trotted a few feet below the peak and there were a couple of rocks to sit on right on the edge of the mountain. I sat on one and relaxed. The crashing of the waves below, the air feeling warm and drowsy and the endless ocean was a bit overwhelming, if not satisfying. My paradise lay before me in all its glory, and I was sated from the grips of humanity. Jim sat down and stared into the waters. His thoughts were silent but on the same wavelength of me. We were here and we had escaped from civilization. My eyes closed and I listened to the melodic symphony below. The sun felt enjoyable on my sweat-dried face. I didn't want to go anywhere else. I didn't want to leave, ever.

We stayed for half an hour or so in silence, and then it was back down the mountain. The first ten feet and my ass was slipping off the side. I missed a step and a slew of rocks and dirt flew down, taking me with them. I turned and grasped at anything I could, knowing if I lost my grip on the mountain, I would be sent to my death. Luckily, I stopped slipping after a couple of feet, but my heart was racing and my mind numb. I turned back around and warily looked below. The crashing rocks smashed into a few thousand pieces and the dirt showered afterward. Beads of sweat gathered on my brow, and I wiped them off quickly on my sweatshirt. It was slow going from here. The only other incident that occurred on our descent was Jim's attempt at payback, when a huge boulder was loosed, and I wasn't aware it was coming at me. He yelled too late, and all I could do is watch it roll down. It rolled down all right, but only a foot next to me. I would have been a pulped orange, if it did hit. We made it down to the bottom. The tide was coming up, and there were a few people walking barefoot on the wet sand. A dog and his master were playing fetch with a stick from the ocean. I had a crazy notion to climb one of the rocks that scraped next to the ocean. It was only twenty feet or so. A jagged, lava-like affair with pinnacles sticking out on all sides. We made it up in two minutes flat. The view from the top wasn't anything spectacular. We spent the rest of the time walking the length of the beach and searching for seashells in the tide pools. As we reached the end of the beach, we looked back at the peak we had just been on, and wondered when we would be back to our seaside oasis.

Two-thirty, and we had to go. It was time to seek out Partington Cove. We drove out of Big Sur proper and drove about six miles south. I saw an inconspicuous gap on the side of the road. There wasn't a No Trespassing sign, and it seemed a place where a trail may be. I started to get excited and ordered Jim to stop the car. He pulled to the side of the road. I hopped out of the car and saw a small dirt trail covered by overgrown weeds and bushes. Aha! I moved quickly, yet cautiously down the trail. It wrapped around a small hill and was fairly level. Hmmm, it wasn't going down. I must have gone about two hundred yards and saw a grave. And then another. These were small handmade graves. A small plaque was represented for each, and some roses were on one. The grave that had the roses showed the date of death one day from today. That was kind of eerie. I walked a little further and the trail went back out onto the highway. It wasn't here. Partington Cove had eluded us again. Jim spooked me when he tapped on my shoulder. We walked back to the graves and looked closer. The person who had died on tomorrow's date was a woman of just 21 years. Tomorrow she would have been dead for a year. A couple of crayon drawn pictures lay at the plaque. The other grave was under a pine tree. The plaque was made of wood and it was a man who had died over ten years ago. The place seemed appropriate for a hidden cemetery. Quiet, peaceful and isolated. We left it and headed back to Lime Kiln.

During the drive back I was killing myself trying to find the elusive Partington Cove. We drove the entire twenty-two miles and I did not see anything until we got to the last bridge before the park. I saw, as I looked back, a trail that looked worn and well used. I also saw a gate that closed off the trail. Hmmm. Maybe we'll check it out tomorrow. We stopped for a few minutes at a small stop and shop called Lucia, and then it was back to the Lime Kiln before the sun went down. We made it to the entrance at four-thirty. We had fifteen minutes before the sunset. We passed the kiosk, drove to the campsite and dumped off our gear and the wood. The forest had gotten quite dark; not dark enough to not see anything, but dark enough to need artificial light. We packed four beers in my backpack and hiked hastily to the beach. We made it just as the sun was starting its descent into the ocean. The skies were a light blue, and wisps of white clouds were stripped across it. The gold orb of warmth turned the ocean waters a pinkish red. I sat down on a small rock and popped open a beer for Jim, and then one for me. The ocean was docile and small waves lapped onto the shore quietly. The light of the last rays of the sun hit the clouds; a smoky orange red hue emanated throughout. The air smelled fresh, and my heart was at ease. I couldn't take my eyes off of the view. Jim stood still, sipping his beer and staring out towards the horizon. The water engulfed the sun and my soul was floating. But only one thing was missing that would have made this perfect. She was 2,000 miles away. I felt a sudden chill inside and a pain in the middle of my chest. I sighed deeply and gulped the beer down. I missed her immensely. The night started to appear and the stars blinked hello. The air got colder and it was time to eat dinner.

We made it back, minus four beers, and stumbled into the campground buzzed and happy. Hot dogs and soup were the main courses for the night. It took us thirty minutes to light a fire. The damn wood was not burning and it was getting pretty dark and cold. After a few thousand matches, and the use of my paper from my notebook as kindling, the fire blazed to life. It was a nice feeling; the flames licking the tops of the grill, and also at my eyebrows. Jim tossed on the hot dogs, and I was the bartender. We ate and ate, drank and drank. I sat on the bench and my glassy eyes stared into the darkness. I could see patches of the night; stars shining brightly and a faint glow of the moonlight. Jim was passing gas and watering the trees every hour. I myself had a few too many beers, and my head felt like a rock. Earlier in the day it could have been a squashed melon. The lullabies of the stream below made my eyelids close. I got up and watered the trees myself. Jim had put out the fire and retired into the tent. I followed soon after, and it was off to a dream world full of water and trees.

I awoke in the early morning, so early that it was still dark. I checked my watch, and through blurred vision I could make out a 5, a 3, and a 4. My head still felt like a ton of bricks, and my body ached. Jim snored happily on my left and I briefly wondered what he was dreaming about. I rolled back over and yawned ever so slightly. My eyelids shut and all I remember before falling back asleep was a loud flagellation next to me.

The next time I got up, I felt a lot better. My head felt pretty light, and I could actually make out the time. It was eight in the morning. The light outside was faint, but noticeable, and with a heave and a-ho I wrenched myself up and took a look around. Jim was still asleep. I heard him mumble something. I couldn't make it out. My breath was visible with the mist of carbon dioxide emanating from my mouth. I got out of my sleeping bag and put on my hiking boots. Then I heard it. A kind of soft, melodic laughter. Unnatural. It was constant, and very pleasing to the ear. I unzipped the tent flap and poked my head outside. I saw nothing unusual. I stepped out and looked around. Nothing. The redwoods were standing in their usual positions, stretching out towards the heavens, and covering the lands with their giant branches. But I noticed that the laughter was louder now. I shuffled to the side of the bank and I found the source of the laughter. The cool water drifted and caressed through the small gorge; its clear and calming visage roaming through rocks eons-old, passing the redwoods on to its final journey to the sea. The bubbling stream. It was the only sound I had heard in all of the forest. Not a car, not an airplane, not a voice. Just the laughter. And I was grateful and lucid to be able to enjoy it for myself. I sat at the bench with my eyes closed and just opened my mind. I felt the same sensation as when I sat on that piece of rock above the ocean yesterday, or when I saw the sunset last night. Total peace, total calm. I was so moved; my eyes welled with tears. After a bit of meditating with nature, I decided to go on a solo hike. Lime Kiln was a very big part of local history. The story goes that lime was smelted and used in the mixture of cement, way back in the late 1800's. What lay in the deep forest were four giant kilns, used to smelt the lime. The lime was then shipped out to sea via donkeys, and then a conveyor line that led to the sea. I grabbed the map and started off.

The trail started right where the bridge crossed the stream. It was fairly new and sturdy. I heard my boots clunk with each step. The trail followed the stream. The incline wasn't very steep, maybe rising a couple of feet every hundred yards or so. The trees started to get denser, the air a chilly fresh. The sunlight poked its rays intermittently through small gaps in the trees and the forest glowed like a doorway to heaven had opened above me. The stream still had its everlasting soothing effect; my steps were light and consistent. I crossed two small bridges. These were the only signs besides the trail itself that represented humanity. I felt like I was in the true wilderness. After about half an hour of hiking in Lothlorien, I happened to see the kilns. They were these four giant brick ovens with rusted steel vents on top of them. The bricks were crumbling. There were some openings to where the lime would be loaded into the kiln. There was even some in there. A fence enclosed the kilns. All I heard was the running water. A bird chirped for a split second. The sun shone down on the kilns to warm the small grove. I kneeled and prayed for a couple of minutes, and then it was back to the campsite.

Jim was not awake when I arrived back. I noisily opened the tent flap and stomped in. Get up! I yelled. A small groan arose from the curled ball of a sleeping bag. It was eight-thirty, time to go. We had a mission. We had to find Partington Cove. It was our destiny. Jim rose and rubbed his eyes. With a quick glance of annoyance at me, he got up. I went outside and started another fire. Everything from last night was burnt out, so I started a two-log fire. This time it started quickly. We made some excellent Earl Grey tea and had bagels smothered in cream cheese along with oatmeal complete with cinnamon and sugar. Everything always tasted better when camping, and this was no exception. We cleaned up as best we could and headed for a quick hike back to the limekilns so Jim could see them and get some morning exercise. After that we headed out of the park and into town; Monterey to be exact. We needed more supplies, as our original plan was to stay one night. But the lure of peace and tranquility had us begging for more. We made the necessary provisions stop at Safeway and a quick call to the car rental agency for another day's use. Then we sped back to Big Sur, our eyes and minds keeping a sharp lookout for the elusive Partington Cove and the so-called 'mystery' path.

We flew back to the point where I had seen the trail, and by God we struck gold. I got out of the car and looked down the gaping gulch below. It was filled with redwoods and the trail wound down to the bottom of, yes, a cove! We went past the gate and followed the sandy switchback trail all the way to the bottom. There were a couple of signs signifying that this was indeed Partington Cove. My mind raced with delight and my body was almost shaking. There was a stream that went towards the sea, and the whole area was covered in redwoods. We crossed a small bridge, and that led to a hundred foot tunnel. It was dank and cold, but sunlight was shining on the other side. We exited the tunnel and had a wonderful view of a secluded cove. The trail was on the right side of the cove and about twenty feet above the water. The ocean lazily swathed its tide in and out of the cove. The water was a beautiful aquamarine and the kelp beds followed the tide's lead. Further to the left was a small rock beach with cliffs above towering above it. There wasn't any way to get in there except by boat. We hiked on the trail for about a couple hundred feet, and then the trail abruptly ended at a bench that was bolted to the white coral ground. There was a wood rail with an opening that led out to the sea that was about twenty yards or so. We carefully walked along the rocky outpost. There were signs of man-made machinery such as a rotting, wooden pulley and rusted screws driven into the rock. Maybe this was a drop-off or pick-up station for abalone or fish. We stood on the edge of the earth, the sea distant for miles. The sun was warm and the breeze cool. There were some tide pools and we saw some anemones and starfish. Most of all there were tons of shell-like clams that were firmly attached to the rocks nearest the waterline. We sat in silence for a while, taking in everything.

The calming effect of the ocean did wonders to my mind. I sighed deeply knowing that though I felt so good and free now, I would have to re-adapt to the crazy and sometimes disheartening life I had back in civilization. It was a sad thing really, that my life felt at ease here in a place where there weren't any humans. I decided to not let the moment pass as a depressing one and I soaked in the experience. Jim seemed to be soaking it in very well. He too was not happy in his life, but this diversion was the perfect medicine, or a perfect cure to what had been ailing him. He had just been in a two and a half year relationship that ended badly. He was still emotionally devastated and was just only starting to heal. I closed my eyes and said a silent prayer that everything would turn out all right. Then it was back to the bridge. There was a fork in the road right at the bridge, and the other trail led to the cove we saw at the top of the highway. It followed the stream all the way until a cropping of rocks appeared. The water ran through them and the trail opened to a white rock beach. Not a soul. I smiled and scrambled up a rock. The waves here were more playful, and some of them crashed heartily against the boulders right at the shore. A spray of white and a sound like thunder. Again and again. We both picked a rock to sit on and proceeded to eat a lunch of bananas, generic lunchables and bottled water. The food tasted good; cheese and turkey on crackers. And for dessert, chocolate chip cookies. The true merging of nature was here. Forest, stream and ocean. After we ate I had a crazy notion. So I found a small pool of stream water and dunked my head in it. My God! The icy water made my face tense up. I pulled my head out and wiped my hair back. It was a baptism of nature. I took off my shirt and walked across the rocks to the other side of the cove. I found a good rock to sit on and meditated, my mind and soul clear. I was alone not for ten minutes, when Jim appeared. His head was wet and he too had baptized himself. Then to have a true baptism of nature, we had to dunk our head in the ocean too. I had found a small tide pool, and when the tide went out, I dunked into the underwater silence. It was just as cold if not colder, than the stream water. But it felt amazing. I felt light. I perched myself on my rock and sunned. No worries, no stress. I heard a splash and Jim finished his baptism as well. We stayed for an hour. I didn't want to leave, but the sun was quick to go down this time of year, so we headed off to the trail. I sadly looked behind me and said farewell to Partington Cove, and vowed to come back soon.

We made it back just in time again. We did the ritual of dropping off the gear, packing the beers and racing to the beach. The sun was well above the horizon and we had visitors this time. A family of three had come to enjoy the sunset with us, and it was nice to actually see more humans than us two. They were an older couple with their adult daughter. They seemed very friendly and though I did not chat with them, Jim did. The water was calm and almost glassy this time. I could make out the black and grey rocks piled against each side of the beach. The highway bridge above us loomed and reminded us that there was a bit of civilization around here. We toasted to better times and happier times, and as our bottlenecks clinked against each other, the sun was going down. Down to the depths of the ocean, never to return. At least for another fourteen hours. This sunset wasn't as fiery and spectacular as yesterday's, but it was nice all the same. The afterglow stayed well after our second beers. Jim walked off and stood next to the shoreline, watching the waves lap onto the shore. I sat back and closed my eyes. When I opened them, Jim was standing right in front of me, slightly startling me. Let's eat, he said. We hiked with the flashlight on and made it back in one piece. It was hotdogs and soup again. We had more beer and the bubbling laughter kept us both company. We talked little. After eating we drank a little more and talked a few minutes about nothing in particular. Jim seemed lost in his own thoughts. I was happily mellow and the stars were again shining through the redwoods. Jim retired for the evening and I stayed up a little longer. After a while of drifting in and out of consciousness, I took my sleeping bag out of the tent and slept outside. The lullabies soothed me to sleep once again and I dreamt of being underwater and floating with the kelp beds and fishies.

Seven-thirty. It was time to get up. I got up with a lurch and remembered I was outside. It was cold and shadowy. The stream welcomed me to a new day. I stretched and stood up to tie my shoes. I swished my mouth with some water and relieved myself at the edge of the cliff. Then it was wakeup time for Jimbo. He got up fairly quickly and we hastily made a fire, and then another breakfast of bagels and oatmeal. Then it was time for the 'ritual'. We had discussed briefly that we would go back to the limekiln sight, and then do the ritual cleansing, which meant that we would strip down naked and submerge our bodies into a small pool of mountain stream water. A sort of bonding with nature kind of thing. We packed some clean clothes and a towel, and we hiked back up to the limekiln sight. It was still as peaceful as ever and I chose the spot that I wished to cleanse myself. It was a small pool of water below a rapid, yet medium-sized waterfall. The water was clean and clear. I stripped off my clothes down to my jockey shorts and took a deep breath. Jim, standing behind me with the camera, was intent to capture the moment on film. I stepped lightly into the water. It was freezing, and I was having second doubts about this. But something inside me told me, if I didn't do this, it showed what kind of person I was. So I waded up to my knees, and then my thighs. My breaths got louder and quicker. And then I closed my eyes and dropped in. I spun around three times to keep my body from going into shock, and at that split second I could have sworn I had a vision of light. I did, however, hear the rushing water from the waterfall resound in my ears. I jumped up and shuffled out of the water. Jim threw me the towel and chuckled. You crazy bastard, he laughed. I nodded and proceeded to dry up. Then Jim stripped down to his boxers. But he didn't go all the way in. He splashed the water on his arms and head, and made a quick exit. We changed and the sun was getting brighter. Its rays shone down from above and filtered through the magnificent redwoods. The limekilns stood tall, seemingly as ancient as the redwoods around us. We hiked back to the campsite and I realized that the vision of light was the camera's flash going off.

We broke down camp fast. The tent was down and packed in minutes and the rest of the gear was stashed back into the trunk. We doused out the fire and kicked the dirt off our boots. It was time to go. I stood one last time near the edge of the water. I listened to the bubbling laughter and it was a part of me now. I took in a mouthful of air and let it out slowly. The rugged redwoods, along with the deep green moss on the rocks, were a picture I kept in my mind. We left behind out temporary sanctuary and drove out of the park. We waved goodbye to the nice old lady in the kiosk and got ready to drive onto the highway. I took a picture of the park sign, and then we flew as fast as the wind on the chipped asphalt. All I could hear now was the bubbling laughter.

Her Ghost

It is a light sort of day. Music plays peacefully in my mind. The bright, clear sky brings out daydreams long lost. A sigh arises from my lungs; my heart skips a beat. I lick my lips from the dryness instilled by the soft warm breezes that dance off my body. She is there. I see her again. The intensity of her bright brown eyes pierce through my own. I know she wants my love. Her soul pulls me towards her, even though my feet do not move. Then, as I get closer and closer, she disappears and fades into nothingness. I frown and look all around me. She isn't anywhere to be found.

Then I feel something touch my back. It feels like a feather has brushed against it. I catch a faint glimpse of auburn as I turn around. I hear a shy laugh. Wisps of air tickle my skin and I feel chilled. But she isn't there.

I awake to the evening cooing of a dove. It is a sad, lonely call to the end of the day. My face feels dry and the air is cool. The sun is sinking westward and the final life of the light desperately spreads itself against the now clouded skies. As if to say, 'I will not go quietly', the rays dance and reflect the mesmerizing orange, pink and purple visions to me. And then I look to my right and she is there. Sitting, her legs pulled up against her body. The white gown she always wore keeping her warm. Her head is perched towards the sky, watching the brilliant display of dying life. Her locks of brown-red floating calmly behind her head. And those piercing eyes full of fire gazing intently above. I can't move, I can't think. All I feel is a deep pain inside the center of my chest so terrible and aching that the love I sought to always contain in my soul drips freely from my eyes. She turns for a brief instant and looks at me. Her beauty is so strong that I can't even move my head and I avert my eyes in shame for showing my feelings. But she smiles. Her face, her eyes, her mouth smile. She moves closer to me, and closes her eyes. She moves her head towards mine, her lips so full of rose blossom I can smell the sweet fragrance, so intoxicating. And just as I can feel her lips touch mine, the light fades away. And so does she.

The stars are keeping me company now. It is quite cold, but the lights in the night sky make me feel just a tad warmer. Misery loves company, perhaps? I imagine the stars as a great light that cannot ever be touched. But as beautiful as they are and how close they seem, you want to reach out and touch them. I close my eyes, and imagine how it would be to feel that warmth that they must have, for certainly anything that can shine as bright as the stars must be warm, even hot. I take in a deep breath of cold night air, and the scent of roses hits my senses again. I purse my lips together tightly. Is she here? I then feel a sudden heat coming from beside me. It becomes very comforting, very welcoming. I turn to my side, and she is lying next to me. Her face is looking straight into the night. The lights of the stars reflect against the softness, paleness of her skin. Do you ever wonder what is up there? She asks me. The same way you wonder what lies in your heart? I reply. She smiles gently and blinks. I still see the passion of life dancing in her eyes. I move my hand towards her face, half-afraid she will disappear, and half-afraid she will disapprove. But neither happens as my hand touches her cheek. It feels so soft, so delicate. It is warm, yet the skin is pale. I slowly run my hand through her hair. Silky and buttery. She closes her eyes and voices her approval with a light groan. Then I suddenly stop. What will happen if you disappear again? I ask. She opens her eyes and looks deeply into mine. What lies in your heart? She answers. I feel the deep pain again inside my chest, the betrayal of feelings arise from my eyes and wash down my face. She closes her eyes and she seems to be waiting for something. I close my own, knowing that even in the dark with my eyes closed, my heart will lead the way. It feels like an eternity of one moment as my lips touch with hers. I can feel her warmth transfer to me, and my body is flush with her essence. Her passion is bringing my dead soul back to life. The emptiness disappears, the loneliness dissipates. The stars keep both of us company.

The light of a new day has brought me new hope. My eyes are bright with life. I feel the need to accomplish what my dreams told me long ago. I breathe in the fresh air, the morning is grateful to be welcomed. I look beside me, and she is still there. She is so beautiful. The morning brightness highlights her face, so peaceful and relaxed. Her chest rises and lowers with each sweet breath she takes in and out. I cannot imagine being with anyone else. I reach to touch her, but she seems to fade. Her body floats away into nothingness. The warmth turns to cold. She is no longer here. But my heart burns with the flame she has given me. And even as my eyes glisten in the light of dawn, I smile and know she is with me.

With Love, From Japan

The doors opened and I saw the sun for the first time in days. My chin itched. It was filled with whiskers. I breathed in the fresh air and felt better. The alarm went off. I was surprised I had woken up before it. I closed the doors and sat down on my bed. Such a cold bed. Such a cold bed.

I took a shower. The hot water felt really good. I washed everything twice. Then I shaved. The cool shaving cream felt good too. The razor did its job well. I looked in the mirror, and saw a man that was 20 years older than he should have been.

I dressed and went to the kitchen. The coffee was already ready. I poured a cup and mixed in cream and sugar. I took a bagel out of the plastic package and went to the refrigerator to get the cream cheese. I felt the cool air. I ate the bagel as if I hadn't eaten in years. The coffee was excellent. I took a look at the empty chair across from me.

I went to the desk where my laptop was. I opened it and waited for it to turn on. Then I clicked on the word processor icon. The words came out like someone breathing. I wrote about her. How she came here. How she stayed. How she left. I shivered a little, so I turned on the heat. Then back to the computer. I typed for an hour. Then I typed for another. I finally stopped when the dog barked. I saw that the mail had been delivered. I saw a letter with a return address from Japan. I put the letter on my desk and let it be. I opened the rest of the mail. Just bills and advertisements. I went back to the kitchen and poured myself a glass of orange juice. It was light and tangy.

Back to the computer. Wrote my memoirs. Those days in San Francisco. All those parties. The bars. The women. The friends who were long gone now. I turned off the computer and went to the living room. It was time to watch the news. Nothing exciting. There was a small earthquake in California. Taxes were going up next year.

My dinner were whiskey and peanuts. Then I abandoned the peanuts. One whole bottle in 3 hours. I turned on the light to my desk and saw the letter. I sat down and sighed. I opened it and it smelled like her perfume. I took the letter out and saw that it was indeed her writing. It said that she missed me. That I should give everything up and come see her. She still loved me. That made me take a long sip from my glass. I put the letter down and wiped my eyes.

I took the phone and dialed long distance. A long, long distance. The phone clicked and I heard, "Mushi mushi?"

"It's me."

"Oh, how are you?"

"I'm doing alright."

"How are you?"

"I'm fine."

"It was a beautiful sunrise this morning. I got your letter. I understood all of it."

71

"Well?"

The money in my pocket jingled. The credit card was next to the bed.

"I wish you came back here."

"I wish that too. But you would love to see Tokyo. It is a wonderful city. And you could write here too!"

I told her that I would be on the next plane. She kissed the receiver and I hung up.

Swimming through a sea of people always made me feel dizzy. But I swam and made it to the airport. I went through all the usual rituals of an airport and finally sat down at my seat, 7C. The plane took off and I saw my city. Goodbye. Goodbye for now.

I wrote some poems on the flight. Love poems. For her. I talked briefly with my fellow passenger. He was going for business. And why are you going? For pleasure. Hope you have a good trip. You too.

The plane landed 16 hours later. I was tired, as I hadn't slept at all. The passengers filtered out of the plane and into the terminal. I was the last to get off. I took my bags and walked slowly. I wanted the anticipation to last. I went through customs. Above the desks there was an observation desk. There she was. In all her beauty. I finally finished all the formalities and stood next to the stairway. I saw her rushing down. She didn't even look at the steps. Her eyes were on me. Then we stood face to face. She put her hand on my cheek. I touched her nose. And that moment lasted forever.

Thursday Night Dinner

The bus arrived on time. I got on, paid my fare, and found a nice comfortable seat near the back. It was the thousandth time I'd taken this trip. Today was no different. The bus actually smelled alright. Usually I would smell either urine or body odor. I guess it was a little different today.

The bus took me to the train station. I got off the bus and saw the usual travelers coming and going from the train station. A well-dressed man with a cropped haircut. A small woman with a wheeled suitcase hailing a cab. And Old Rusty. I never knew his name, but I always saw him at the entrance. He wore a black knit skull cap, had a few days growth on his face and a look of sadness in his eyes. His main aim was twofold. One, to get money from anyone who would give it to him. He would hold out his dirty hand and ask for change. Nobody saw him. He was invisible. The second thing was cigarettes. He never asked for them, even from people who were smoking, but he would look for butts on the ground. Just a little more nicotine for a lost soul. I felt sorry for him. Sometimes we would make eye contact, but most of the time he most likely would be looking down. God bless him.

I smoked my cigarette in silence. Then I went to Subway, which was inside the train station, and got a roast beef sandwich. Today was a bad luck day for sandwiches, as when I went back outside to eat it, it fell from the wrapping and the meat touched the ground. With nobody looking, I gathered the meat off the ground and put it back into the bread. I took a bite and it tasted good. Maybe I wasn't as different as Old Rusty as I thought I was.

The train docked into the station, and I bought my ticket. One-way, and to zone four. $4.50. I got out the exact change and put it into the machine. The machine groaned a couple times, and then spit out my ticket. The doors opened to the waiting train and I walked with the countless other travelers and went to the train. I got on the last car. They usually never checked your ticket on the front and back parts of the train. I always hated digging for the ticket in my pocket. I found a seat on the top part. I sat down and relaxed. I had an hour and a half until I reached San Jose.

I usually picked the right side of the car, because the sun would shine on the left side. And it was unbearable. And there was a better view on the right side of the car. The train conductor announced we would be leaving momentarily and that we should keep our feet off the chairs. We would be making all the stops en route to San Jose. Make sure you have your ticket ready for the conductor. The train started rolling on the track. First it lurched, as if it had found a stone on the ground and tripped on it. Then it started to get smoother. We were off.

I never did anything special on the train ride. Sometimes I would read a magazine or a book, but most times I would sleep. I couldn't concentrate on the words when people were talking. And there was always a couple, a family, even a solitary man talking, either with each other or by themselves. And also those cell phone talkers. So I would drift in and out of sleep, sometimes looking out the window to see which city we were coming to. The only thing waking me up would be the conductor's voice over the intercom, announcing the coming destination. Today, I slept without interruption. Not even the monotone of the conductor's voice bothered me.

We finally made it to San Jose. I got off the train and walked outside the train station. My bus stop was nearby. I lit up another cigarette and enjoyed it immensely. A cute young woman walked by. She smiled at me. I waited until she left and I smiled to myself. Not ugly yet. Not disgusting yet. Still young. Still young. I walked to the bus stop and sat down. The bus came a few minutes later and I got on. I saw trees with no leaves. Wet gutters still siphoning last night's rain. Expensive cars on the road.

I have never met anyone on the train or the bus. I saw different people all the time. An older lady clutching her purse. A couple teenagers gossiping about their classmates. A fat man trying to fit into one seat. I always blotted out the chatter and noise. Probably because I would be seeing my family at the end of the destination. And that made me happy.

The bus stopped at my stop. I got off and started the short walk to my parent's house. It smelled clean. Fresh and cool. I walked through a neighborhood that I had walked through countless times. Today there weren't any people, families or kids out. Then when I got close to the house, I saw my best friend's mom walking their dog. He was a collie. She waved to me, and I waved back. We talked for a few minutes and she seemed happy. I told her I would call Lance tomorrow. Tell everyone I said hi. Same here. She walked off and I headed full steam to the house.

My mom opened the door. Kelani muscled her way to the front and she was wagging her tail like crazy. I walked inside and greeted my mom. Then I took Kelani out to the back and hugged her. I petted her. She licked my hands, arms and face. I always had to take her outside because sometimes she would pee, being so excited. This time she did not. I went back inside and put my bag in the computer room. I sat down on an easy chair in the living room. Baseball was on the TV. My dad was in his room. He came out and he nodded to me. I checked my mail in a box my mom had for me near the door. Student loan notices. Bills. A couple literary magazines. And an ad for a free cruise to the Bahamas. I wondered if that one was genuine or not.

I talked to my mom for a bit. I told her that the writing was going well. I was writing every day and getting out every day. I was enjoying my time in San Francisco. She asked if I was eating well. I lied and said yes. Actually I was only eating once a day. And a small meal at that. No worries though. I wasn't that hungry nowadays.

It was 7 pm, and soon I would see the rest of the family. My mom called my sister Erin and asked what she wanted for dinner. What did the kids want? Then she asked me and my dad. I heard the front door open a couple minutes later and it was my sister Andrea, my brother-in-law Raymond, and my littlest and youngest nephew Diego. Diego was a fun kid. He was two years old, and had brown eyes and brown hair. He looked like a miniature person. He spoke

77

three languages. English, Spanish and Hawaiian. He was just starting to make sentences. Andrea told him to say hi to me, and to give me a hug. I grabbed the little guy and held him in my arms. I gave him a kiss on his cheek and let him go. He found his toy box and started playing with an Elmo doll. I shook Raymond's hand and hugged Andrea. It was good to see them, since I only saw them once a week, sometimes once a month.

We were all sitting in the living room, waiting for Erin and my nephews and niece to come to the house. The baseball game was over, and a college football game came on. Dad and Raymond talked about sports and work. Andrea talked about Diego to my mom. I watched Diego, as he started playing with a train now. He looked happy and healthy. That's all we could ask for.

Erin came to the house a little after 7:30 pm. Someone opened the front door, but I couldn't see who it was. Then my niece Malia popped in front of the door. She was six years old, but looked like ten. She was the youngest of Erin's children. She had dirty blonde hair that was always in a ponytail and blue-green eyes. She didn't look Asian or African American at all, except for the shape of her eyes. They were almond-shaped. She was always happy and cheerful. She went straight for Diego. Then came my middle nephew Jordan. Now 8 years old, he looked hapa. He had slight Asian features and dark skin. A little more reserved, he waved to everyone and had a toy in his hand. Finally my nephew Darrien walked through the door. He was fourteen and a true teenager. He was in high school and played basketball and football. He was almost six feet tall and was the tallest of all the family except for his stepdad. He was the quietest one of all, but a loveable kid. He didn't say anything and sat down next to my dad.

My mom, Andrea and I went to McDonald's to get dinner. The story about this is this; when my mom first started working at Intel, she would buy dinner on Thursday nights. And it was always McDonald's. This tradition went on for over 30 years, and it was still going strong. There were some Thursday nights over the years when we didn't do this because of other obligations or emergencies, and there were times when we moved the time of the week to another day, but it was still a regular thing. We made it to the restaurant and my mom ordered for the whole family except for Andrea. Andrea ordered her food separately and we sat down to wait for our orders to be filled. Andrea went outside to get a Metro newspaper. About ten minutes later our orders were ready.

I had the twenty piece McNuggets, a large fries and a large Sprite. The kids always got happy meals except Darrien. Darrien had moved from little kid to an adolescent, so he ordered what the adults got. He usually got a McChicken sandwich. But this time he got a couple of wraps and a large fries. He loved shakes, so my mom got him a strawberry shake. Everyone else got what they wanted, and before we went to our respective places to eat, we held hands in a circle and prayed over dinner.

After dinner, it would be time to spend time with the kids. Diego was most content playing with his toys, and as long as he was in seeing distance of my sister and/or brother-in-law, he was fine. Jordan would go to the back bedroom and watch a movie. Darrien went to the game room to play on the Xbox. I spent most of my time with Malia. She loved playing board games, and my parents had a multi-board game box. First we played chutes and ladders. That was Malia's favorite. When we finished playing that, we would play Chinese checkers. I longed to show her how to play chess. But she was not ready for that yet. I would talk with her too. I asked her if she made any new friends. Asked her if she was doing well in school. She seemed well and happy, and that was good. She was a smart kid.

When we finished playing games, we went to see Jordan. He was watching Kung Fu Panda. He was laughing at all the jokes and slapstick. I sat next to him and Malia lay on the bed. We watched for a few minutes. Jordan put his head on my lap. Malia put her arms around my neck. We enjoyed this time together and I was extremely happy. When Jordan talked, you listened because he didn't talk much. In between scenes, he would tell me that he got a green sticker, which meant that you were a good child that day. He also told me that he was going to play flag football soon, t-ball in the spring. He was probably the smartest kid of all of them. He was left-handed just like my dad and me. All lefty.

Darrien always played NBA 2K12 on the Xbox. When we got bored of watching the movie with Jordan, Malia and I would go see Darrien. He was engrossed with the game, but had time to talk as well. I asked him how football was going. He wasn't playing, but enjoyed wearing the pads and uniform. When he played basketball, he would definitely be playing. He had been playing basketball since he was little, and was always a good player. No girlfriends yet. He was the quiet type, so I never asked him about that. He had a report due next week, and a poem to recite in two weeks. That made me happy. Glad to hear they hadn't abandoned poetry in high school.

My mom made ice cream cones for the kids after dinner had settled. When they ate, I played with Diego. He was always running around, playing with his toys and laughing at my dad. My dad would mock chase him around the house, and Diego loved this. He was obsessed with the movie Cars, and everything about it. He wanted to see the movie. He wanted to talk about Lightning McQueen and Mater. He even had Cars toys and a Cars brochure. If he could read, he would have read the Cars picture book. He usually hung out with me for a little bit, and then went to do something else. I always made sure to spend time with all of my nephews and niece.

Time to go home. My dad would go to bed, and then soon thereafter everyone would go. First Andrea, Raymond, and Diego. Andrea would change Diego into his pajamas and give him his night bottle. After he was finished, my brother-in-law would carry him and lean him towards me so I could give him a kiss goodnight. Then they left. Erin left next with the rest of the kids. We all hugged goodbye. Malia would hug me the hardest. Jordan would stand limp as I hugged him. And Darrien would hover over me with his tall, lanky body and hug me with one arm. I always felt sad when everyone left. Mom and I would watch a little more television. And then it would be my turn to leave. Mom drove me to the bus stop, and I would think about my family as I waited for the bus. The bus came and I got on. Then it was the long haul back to San Francisco.

Middle East War

I am writing today to address the situation in the Middle
East and my personal opinion on it according to my
observations based on television, the radio and the Internet.
First of all, I am a news junkie and the first television
station/radio station/webpage I always go to will be CNN. I
am usually greeted with small domestic news and maybe a
smidgen of international news that may or may not be of
importance. Like the other day, I saw the unfolding news of
the Yugoslavian elections. It was an important and defining
moment in history. I was listening and watching every
word and picture that had significance to the events that
were happening there. Seeing Kostunica being sworn in as
the president of the FRY was very moving in the fact that I
believed that it would be years before the situation would
change for the better there. And so history was made. After
that, nothing very exciting happened except for some little
incidents in a place called Israel. And then the ball started
rolling downhill. I was horrified at the culmination of the
violence that had erupted there when I awoke to scenes of
Israeli reserve soldiers being 'lynched' by a Palestinian
mob of perhaps forty to fifty people. A young man raised
his hands to reveal the blood on them, his patriotic duty of
destroying all that is Jewish was accomplished. Then the
body flying out of the second story window; the mob
chanting with terrifying alacrity as they stomped and
stabbed and kicked at the either helpless soldier or
discarded corpse, as I don't know whether the soldier was
dead or not. I sighed and felt quiet anguish in my heart. I
was troubled once again that the human race had stooped so

low to its animal instinct of violence. I was glued to the television, watching the events of the rest of the day unfold. The retaliation by the Israel government, with missiles flying and slamming into buildings. Explosions that rocked the immediate areas, sending debris everywhere. The light of the fantastic fires that had started seemed to look like some sort of hastily created hell. People scrambling for their lives. And again my mind became numb with the barren, yet painful fact that humanity was indeed still a young baby.

Anger was my initial reaction. Why? Why was this happening? I was losing faith in the human being. I couldn't have the same blood, bones, skin and human features of those animals on the television screen. But I did. It was the mind and mentality that was different. But perhaps if I were oppressed and had my respect as a living human taken away from me on a daily basis, then maybe, just maybe, a reaction that had happened to those soldiers could be a viable incident. For anyone, but for me? I had to look deep down inside myself, and see if I wasn't just kidding myself.

Early evening, and I had been exhausted by the news that was filtered to the USA. And then something happened that made me open my eyes more wide than ever. Ehud Barak, the Prime Minister of Israel, was being interviewed on CNN. He looked tired and angry. The interview lasted for about ten minutes, with Mr. Barak answering each question with passion. Most of the questions were based on the violence of the day and if the peace process were dead or not. I had thought that Mr. Barak would take the stand of his predecessors by locking the Palestinians in their self-governed lands and say, 'Well, that's it. It's over.' It's over, meaning that the peace process was dead and that there weren't going to be any changes to that policy in the future. What struck me most was that though Mr. Barak was indeed angry at the deaths of the Israeli soldiers and how it was done, he did not give up the notion that the peace process was dead. Nor did he make the Palestinian people responsible for the faltering toleration of Jews.

AMANPOUR: There's so much anger. Do you really think there is room to restart the peace negotiations?

BARAK: Yes. There will always be room. We will never lose hope of peace. The Palestinian people are going to be our neighbor forever; we will make peace with them. Leadership can change its mind, leadership can open its eye and leadership can even be replaced. And we might lose trust and hope of this present leadership, but we will never lose the hope of having peace with our Palestinian neighbor, the same people who are innocently pushed or incited to go into these demonstrations.

This was a part of the transcript that was the interview between Prime Minister Ehud Barak and CNN correspondent Christiane Amanpour. When Mr. Barak answered this question, he said it in a passionate, positive way that actually took me by complete surprise. It told me that Mr. Barak had not given up on peace. It told me that this man was more than I thought he was. It actually gave me shivers and my eyes watered. Perhaps there is some room for debate on the issue of being human.

After that interview, I was done with it. I couldn't take it anymore. I sat down and drank a beer and watched a soccer game. I had much to think about. But what stuck in my mind for the next few hours was: We will never lose hope of peace.

A La Seattle

Day One

With Jim leering at the female flight attendant's behind most of the flight, I slept most of the two-hour flight to Seattle. It was mid-April, and having the travel lust that flowed through me every so often, my mind came to Seattle. I had not been to Seattle before, but there were many things that I was interested in seeing there. My first and foremost interest was the famed Pike Place Market, a world renowned produce market that not only sold fruits, vegetables, fish (also world renowned) and other produce, but also the small, antiquated shops that had everything from classic rock and roll tour posters to trinkets probably found at the bottom of the ocean. Also, I was keen on the sports teams there; The Mariners, Seahawks, and Supersonics. Last, but not least, were the micro-beers. I was a connoisseur and beer snob, and Seattle was famed for its diversified and tasty brews. Coffee did not even enter my mind. Or Nordstrom's for that matter. So I dragged poor Jim along with me, and though the trip was cost-conscious, we planned to spend a bit.

We landed at Sea-Tac Airport and rushed through the terminal to get our bags and find the local transportation that would take us into downtown Seattle. The airport itself was sparse of taste, but clean, and we walked to the end of the rental car desks to find the exit to the place. Not a soul was stirring; there wasn't even a security guard around. I looked at my watch and it read 10:30 am. Then Jim spotted an automatic door and we stepped out. The first thing to hit us was the rain. I had heard that Seattle was a wet place, and its reputation did not disappoint us as sheets came down and splattered all over us. The clouds were thick and gray, and if we even attempted to sit at the bus stop bench, we would have been drenched quickly. We hurriedly went back into the airport, and watched through the window, waiting for the bus to come. Jim's green army jacket was soaked and my long black hair was dripping. I pushed it back and shook my head. We looked like a couple of homeless guys standing around waiting for something to happen. The bus arrived soon enough though, and we sprinted for the door before the bus driver could close it on us. He seemed like he didn't want to stop, but I guessed he saw us peering out from inside the airport. We hopped on and sat in the back. The bus was not packed. Actually, there were only three people on it besides Jim and I. A young man was reading a textbook to the front left of the bus; an elderly Chinese woman was sitting directly across from the bus driver clutching some paper bags; a black man was reading a newspaper, about halfway to the right. Jim took off his jacket and shook it. The damn guy sprayed me with the water and I cursed at him. He shrugged and sat down. I took out my guidebook and looked at our next destination-The Moore Hotel.

The Moore Hotel, unbeknownst to Jim and I, was old and famous. It was a hotel that was known for The Moore Theater, a famous entertainment venue that had been in Seattle for many years. From what my guidebook told me, the rates were good, and the only other affordable places was the Commodore Motor Hotel (which sounded that it rented by the hour), that was a block away, and The St. Regis, a hotel catering to recovering alcoholics and drug addicts. We opted for The Moore. We didn't see too much when we came in from I-5 and into Seattle proper, but the world famous Space Needle was visible from the sparse skyline, and we did pass by the Kingdome, an indoor arena that was home to The Seattle Mariners baseball team and The Seattle Seahawks NFL franchise. The bus stopped on 2nd Avenue, and we had to walk up a block to the Moore. It was a whitewashed, semi-tall building. There was an adjoining café next door, and the theater was to the left of the hotel. We walked through the revolving glass door and went up to the desk. The lobby smelled like old cigarettes, and the scenery was quite drab, with puke-green carpet stained by who-knows-what and plastic chairs and a table. The table was overloaded with magazines. I went up to the reception desk, and there was a thick eye-glassed man typing on an old typewriter. There was an egg salad sandwich half-eaten next to the typewriter, and a steaming Styrofoam cup of coffee on the desk. White paint was chipped off the desk, and other than the coffee, it was bare. I inadvertently kicked the desk with my leather hiking boot and the man got up with a start. He mumbled something incoherent, and he asked for my name. I told him. He shuffled through some papers and found my reservation. It was forty dollars a night. Between the two of us, twenty. We paid two nights and he gave me a key to room 5A. Fifth floor, room A. We grabbed our bags and found the elevator. It had wooden doors and it squeaked badly. When we entered the elevator and pushed the grimy button for the

fifth floor it seemed we were in slow motion, as the
elevator seemed to be moving in. We finally reached the
coveted fifth floor and walked onto the same puke-green
carpet that lined the hallway. 5A was right there to our left
and we had no trouble getting into the room.

The first thing I noticed about the room was the ceiling.
The damn thing must have been at least fifteen feet high,
and I kept gaping at it periodically while checking out the
rest of the room. Jim thought I was feeling inferior because
of the height of the room. Ha-ha. There were two queen-
sized beds with the same (they must have gotten a great
deal for the color coordination perhaps) puke-green colored
comforters that covered the mattresses. A twist knob
television sat on top of a fake wooden stand, and there was
the nightstand between the two beds. One lamp was
attached to the wall above the nightstand and there were
some brown (surprise!) curtains that were closed. Lastly,
there was a small round table with two chairs near the
window. I threw my backpack on my bed, nearest to the
door and Jim sat down at the table. He seemed quite
satisfied with the accommodations. I had been in worse.

Our agenda was pretty tangible, so if either one of us
wanted to check out something, then most likely we would
go see it. There were some must-sees, and they would in
turn be seen. It was Wednesday in the late morning and we
had to leave on a six-thirty morning flight on Friday. The
first task we set ourselves upon was to eat. We were both
famished, and all we had to eat all morning were those
small packages of peanuts and a four ounce drink that was

complimentary on the airplane flight. We walked out of the hotel and decided that we would find a place near Pike's Place Market, so we could start the sightseeing there. The rain had stopped and it was partly cloudy overhead. Patches of deep blue could be seen and even the sun shone in small amounts. With the weather changing, I was getting warm. I stripped off my raincoat and put it in my backpack. We walked down Virginia Street and that led us down toward the waterfront. We walked around for a while, not particularly looking at things, but the streets were moderately crowded with people and there were cars coming and going. We settled on a restaurant called Queen City Grill. It was on top of a small retail clothes store. It was a nice place, the prices weren't bad, and the menu had some excellent fare. And there was a view of the water from our table. We basically scarfed down our food like a bunch of savages, and when we finished, we tipped the cute waitress an extra ten percent.

Pike Place Market. Though I didn't know too much about it, I did know that it was varied and stylish to go there. It was only a short distance from where we ate, and in no time we were there. A giant neon sign with the words, 'Pike's Place Market', was on top of the main part of the market, and at the end of the street, which had a left turn only, there was the famed fish market. Long display cases filled with almost every local fish imaginable was there. We even got to see the famous 'fish tossing' that the salesmen did for the customers. One guy would be behind the counter, and another guy in front of the counter, about ten feet away, tossed fish from an ice filled crate. The fish tosser would yell 'Fish coming!', and he would fling the fish over the counter with authority. The guy on the other side of the counter would catch it with both hands and put it in the display cases. And these fish they were flinging and catching were not small. They were at least two feet long, and maybe ten pounds apiece. We watched this cool spectacle for a little bit, then ventured into the market itself. It basically was like a mini-mall, with small shops that varied from children's clothes, antiques, candy, and an arcade that featured an impressive pinball machine row and skeet ball lanes. We took a look around for a while, and when we lost interest, we decided to go to the waterfront and take a look at the water.

The water was glassy and dark, not at all an incredible sight for the eyes, but it was another view of the Pacific Ocean I hadn't seen before. There wasn't anything special about the view except in the distance there were a couple of islands and there was also a ferry way off coming towards us. Jim was getting bored quickly, so I asked him if he wanted to head for the breweries. He was so excited that he almost jumped five feet up into the air. We looked at the map, and just a few stores down the waterfront was a place called Pike Place Brewery. We walked for a couple of minutes and we found the brewery. It wasn't hard to see; it was two stores in one, and there was a red, white and blue sign that said, 'Pike Place Brewery'. We rushed into the brewery and the place really was a small microbrewery. There was a gigantic copper vat, many brewing supplies, and an area where you could make your own beer. But we were looking for the beer itself, and there was the homemade tap ready to serve at a small, makeshift bar. The crusty old man behind the bar counter eyed us suspiciously, and we had to flash our I.D.s to be able to buy the alcoholic brew. We downed two pints rapidly, and the taste was divine. It was bitter with a sweet aftertaste. Quite different and unique. The alcohol went to my head fast and I was buzzing pretty well. Jim had a perpetual smile on his face, and he wanted to check out the Seattle Center, which was a fair ways away from where we were. On the way over, we saw the famous Spoonman. He was a bald, tattooed man who played music with a couple of spoons. He was very fast and very talented. Soundgarden immortalized him with song for him called 'Spoonman'.

We walked back up the waterfront, passed a few piers, and made a right on Vine Street. When we intersected 2nd Avenue, it was like we stepped back into the past. The streets were super clean and empty and there were those old hanging stoplights that were suspended by a wire. It was a change compared to the more modern area of Seattle that we had just been around. We walked down 2nd Avenue, and we happened upon a store. It was a hockey store. Jim, the great sports fanatic, begged me to go in. I had no qualms, so we went in. The place looked like a normal sports souvenir store with jerseys hanging on carousels, hats sporting the logos of the hockey teams and posters galore of various hockey stars. I was looking at some hockey cards at the front when Jim waved me over to a clothes carousel. He pulled out a hockey jersey that I did not recognize. It had a bald eagle on it and it had the name, 'Thunderbirds', on it. I knew most of the NHL hockey teams, but this team did not sound familiar. We walked up to the front and a red mustachioed man wearing an identical hat of the same logo as the jersey was talking on the telephone. I looked down at the display case as we waited and there were also hockey pucks and pins next to the cards. The man got off the telephone and asked us if we needed anything. We asked him about The Thunderbirds and he chuckled. You aren't from around here, are you? He proclaimed. We both nodded like a couple of dumb tourists, and he proceeded to tell us that it was Seattle's ice hockey team. They were in a junior (semi-pro) hockey league called The WHL, or Western Hockey League. Aha! In fact, he told us, the team had reached the conference playoffs and there was a game on tonight at the Seattle Center. We immediately bought two tickets and I bought a hockey puck with the Seattle Thunderbirds logo on it. Jim bought a hockey puck as well and the jersey he had brought up front with him. We thanked the guy and headed out to The Seattle Center.

It took us about twenty minutes to reach the center and it was midafternoon by then. The skies had cleared, but the ground was still slick with the recent rains. The air was getting a little colder as well. The Seattle Center was a complex of buildings that had The Coliseum, where the basketball team The Supersonics played, a small amusement park called Fun Forest, a gigantic fountain called International Fountain, one end of the monorail, and the world famous Space Needle. As we got closer and closer to the needle, the more and more it looked impressive. It poked into the wispy clouded sky, and it was nice; not a sore sight on the eyes. We walked into the center complex and the first thing we saw was the fountain. Though it was not spouting water at the moment, it was a sight to see. It was about thirty feet around and it was in a trough. There were many holes that went around the circumference, and a large pool in the middle. I guessed when it was on the water would shoot through the holes while the middle was the fountain proper. The fountain was in the middle of a cement courtyard and a ring of flagpoles surrounded the courtyard. On each flagpole there was a flag of various nations. On one side of the courtyard there was the Coliseum, which was closed. On the opposite side of the courtyard there was a place called Center House, a small collection of shops and eateries for tourists. We went and looked around there for a bit and I ended up buying some t-shirts for my sisters.

We wandered around the center and saw the small amusement park, which had a mini-roller coaster, a Ferris wheel and a carousel. Some game booths completed the amusement park's attractions. There weren't many people around, probably because it was a weekday, but there was a scattering of kids with their moms going here and there. Some large statues dotted the center and one was a fifteen-foot statue of an army soldier armed and ready. I hopped up and held onto his leg while Jim took a picture. By then, we were hungry and we wanted to ride the monorail. We went to the empty line, bought a ticket for ninety cents and hopped on. It was a smooth, quick ninety-second ride from the Seattle Center to Westlake Center and we went inside Westlake to find some food. Hamburgers and fries ended up being dinner for us, and we sat at an open-air café watching television. Westlake was your typical mall, with clothes shops and restaurants. It wasn't anything eye-opening. After dinner, it was back to the monorail, so we could catch the hockey game, which started at seven-thirty. The sun had already gone away and the cold came in quickly. I put my raincoat back on as the clouds were getting thicker up above. So far I had to say it was a nice start to seeing Seattle, though it wasn't as spectacular as I had hoped. Jim, however, seemed mesmerized by the Emerald City, and he would comment every so often about this or that and how it was cool.

The hockey game started fast and furious, as The Seattle Thunderbirds were playing The Kamloops Blazers for the sixth game of a best of seven conference playoffs. The crowd was blue collar and rowdy and my ears were burning from the epithets and insults hurled at the opposing team. The players crashed each other into the boards with ferocious velocity and a few fights broke out. At one point in the second period, a Kamloops player chased behind a Thunderbirds player with his hockey stick raised above his head, intent to strike him on the head. The game ended in regulation tied and it went into overtime. By then, I was part of the crowd yelling and cursing, getting into the spirit of the atmosphere. Jim was also animated and yelling. It was an adrenaline rush. Sports combat. How fabulous. The Thunderbirds won the game with an overtime goal and the series was tied 3-3. When we left the ice rink there was a long line at the ticket office to buy tickets for the deciding Game 7. The air was cold, but it tasted fresh and welcome compared to the heated battleground we had just left. We were on our way back to the hotel, but there was one last place we had to go before we went back- The Needle.

We wanted to go on top of The Space Needle at night because we wanted to see the city lighted up at night. It was open until one in the morning, and when we headed towards it, the time was eleven. It must have rained while we watched the hockey game because the ground was wet. A small wind had picked up as well. We entered the metal masterpiece and took the elevator to the top level. We stopped once to drop off some diners at the restaurant that was on the structure, and then we got to the top. As soon as we got out of the elevator, we walked right into its second restaurant, which was a revolving restaurant. There was an exit door to the observation deck, and as soon as I opened the door a burst of frigid air hit both Jim and I. We hastily went out and shut the door. The deck was wet and windy as hell. But the view was fascinating. On the south side, you could see downtown Seattle with its lights bright and luminous, and behind it an awesome sight of Mount Rainier towered behind it. The peak was coated with snow and it was just one gigantic volcanic cone. I stood there looking at it for quite some time until Jim nudged me to move around the deck. We moved clock-wise and saw the blackness of Elliott Bay; the great Pacific Ocean a dark abyss. Then we saw the suburbs of Seattle, with the lights of cars driving along the streets. I took a picture of Jim standing next to the rail and my hands could barely keep hold of the camera as the wind bit at my fingers. The picture ended up looking hilarious, as Jim's hair was blown straight up and his coat was whipping around his body. He was clutching a couple of newspapers that seemed to look like they were about to take flight. He complained later that he would never let me talk him into going up on The Space Needle in that weather again. I laughed heartily.

Day Two

DAMN! The white light penetrated through my eyelids and stung my irises. I threw the covers over my head. Ahhhhhh, darkness. All of a sudden the light came back and it hurt even worse. And it was cold. Jim had pulled the covers from me. Damn Jim. I opened my eyes slowly and gave him the evil eye. He laughed at me and sat down at the desk. He watched the news on the television while I got up and went to the bathroom. I looked at my watch. It was six in the morning. My God. I took a quick shower and brushed my teeth. We had a long day ahead of us.

Sitting at the Moore café, staring drowsily at my coffee, Jim proceeded to plan out the day for us. We were to go to the Seattle Kingdome and try to get in on a tour, and then go to Pioneer Square and check that area out. Afterward, we would play it by ear. I munched a little on the stale toast, and drank the weak black coffee. We headed out into the chilly, yet clear Seattle morning and were off.

First, we went to get some cash at the closest ATM. Then we caught the free local bus transportation and took it all the way to the south side of Seattle to The Kingdome. We got there in ten minutes, and when we exited the bus, there was The Kingdome. It looked like it was falling apart.

The panels on the top of the dome were dilapidated and even some were being replaced. The sounds and voices of the workmen on top of the dome could be heard. We looked around the place and tried to find an office or someone who could get us into the sports field. After a couple of minutes of walking around the dome and avoiding giant mud puddles, we saw a sliding door that opened into the dome. There was a security booth next to it and a couple of guards were talking while drinking coffee. I peered in and you could see the dark green of the artificial turf stand out against the shadows. You could barely see anything except the turf, and the closer we got, the guard's attention turned to us. We asked if there was a tour, and they said they usually did have tours, but because they were currently renovating the building for the upcoming season, no tours were being scheduled. Damn it. Just our luck. We were twenty feet from being able to go into the place and we were denied. I asked if maybe we could take a couple of pictures near the entrance of the open door and he frowned. Not without authorization, he said. He talked into his walkie-talkie and after a minute or so, he ushered us near the door. No going inside, he cautioned us. Jim stood about a couple of feet into the stadium and I took a couple of pics. Then I went closer to take a look inside. Now the place looked a little clearer. The overwhelming sense I got was that the place was spacious. The seats were on three levels and I could make out the baseball diamond. The bases weren't in place, but home plate was visible. Though we didn't get to see all that we wanted to, we were satisfied.

After the Kingdome, we walked under the I-5 overpass and into Pioneer Square. Pioneer Square was an older part of Seattle, but it was known for its hip restaurants and plentiful bookstores. We walked down the red brick streets and looked around. It wasn't crowded at all and we took our time enjoying the various stores that were around. We went into an antique store that also doubled as an art gallery, and the main theme was the ocean. Paintings of boats on stormy seas and water creatures swimming underwater were hanging from the clean, white walls. There were a couple of old relics from ships; a giant anchor that was perched on a two-foot stand; a brass hurricane lamp that looked brand new; a sextant that looked like it was made of copper. The music playing in the store was one of those new age kind of deals, and it was a pleasant store to be in. Then we walked further and saw The Elliot Bay Book Company, and we went in. This was Seattle's crown jewel of bookstores, and the place did not disappoint. It felt very relaxing and mellow, with its redwood floors and rows upon rows of books labeled by subject. It was fairly busy, but to my surprise it wasn't loud like some department store; it was more like a library. A young lady with short blonde hair asked if we needed any help, and I asked where the travel section was. She ushered me into a quaint corner with one long bookshelf, and left me to my own business. I looked up and down the shelf and finally picked out a book on the Pacific Northwest. Then I sat down in the chair that was tucked in the corner. Jim disappeared, and I read a bit of the book I was about to buy. It was a history type of book, with some stories included.

Then Jim showed up showing me a Calvin and Hobbes cartoon collection and he was pointing out the funny ones. We bought our books and decided it was time for lunch. We walked up and down the streets and finally picked a restaurant called Umberto's Ristorante. It was a trendy type of Italian restaurant with some art pieces hanging on the bright, colored walls and jazz playing on the speakers. I ordered chicken with pasta and Jim ordered linguini with clams. And we each had a pint of the local brew on tap. We struck up a conversation with our waitress and she told us that on Thursdays, which was today, the locals would go jazz hopping. That meant people would go to each of the little hole-in-the-wall jazz clubs and frequent two, three, four or as many clubs they could manage. I think Jim took to her, as he kept on looking at her more than eating his lunch. I laughed to myself and ordered another pint. When we left, Jim left a twenty-dollar bill and I was almost tempted to swipe it, but I didn't.

We took a quick look at the Waterfall Garden, which was a small park that had a myriad of waterfalls all over. It was peaceful, but we were rushing to get to the art museum before it closed. On the way back to the bus stop, we saw a couple of bicycle police busting two vagrants and we got constantly panhandled upon by the homeless who were finally awake. We took the bus to the Seattle Art Museum, and we got off one stop too early. I was ready to hit Jim over the head with my book bag, but I thought better of it. He had the hotel room key. We walked a block down and got into the museum. It was open for a few more hours, so we took our time looking around. Most of the museum was not a strictly art gallery type of museum. They had displays that were theme-oriented; there was a section with ancient Chinese artifacts and relics. That was really interesting as some of the pieces dated way back into the ancient Ming Dynasty and earlier. There was also a section that dealt with colonial drinking mugs, and there were many different types of flagons and tankards made of pewter and silver. But the museum was otherwise unimpressive, and we took our leave after half an hour.

At this time, we were getting tired, so we wanted to go somewhere that was close by and that did not deal with strenuous activity. Jim suggested we go to the Omnidome. It was a massive theater that played a short film of the history of Mt. Saint Helens and its unfortunate end in 1980. That sounded pretty good, so we walked back down towards the waterfront and it was easy to find because the dome-like structure was situated right at the waterfront itself. We waited in line with about a thousand kids and their moms, and when we got inside we sat down in a theater-like room. The chairs were comfortable and the screen was gigantic. I don't think it was more than 70MM, but it was large enough. The movie was very well done, but I only caught a few minutes, as the lack of sleep and the beers made me drowsy and sleepy when the lights went out. I awoke with a start when on the screen the whole sequence of Mt. Saint Helens exploding and decimating the land it was on came on. It was horrifying and awesome at the same time. That was the end of the movie. When we left the theater, they passed out some single slides of the explosion of the volcanic cone, and a paper with a stamp on it signifying the authenticity of the slide. The sun was pale and the air was getting colder. Evening was coming. We decided it was time to look for dinner.

Ivar's Fish Bar was not only a historic landmark of Seattle history, but it was also one of Seattle's oldest fast food restaurants. Serving up hot fish and chips and other fried seafood was its specialty and we decided that it would be a fitting dinner and last meal in Seattle. It was only a couple of blocks down from the theater, so we walked down the waterfront and felt the sting of the sea air whip into our jackets and through our skins. The place was an open-air restaurant that was painted blue and white with a picture of a Viking's ship atop the restaurant. We got there right before it got busy, as after we ordered our food, a crowd of people came and ordered theirs. The poor cook in back was new and he was rushing and sweating to get all the orders done. I sat down at a covered table and Jim waited to pick up the food. The rain started to come down right when Jim brought the food to the table. He handed me a red basket full of chips with a large, crisp piece of fish on top. Jim had a basket of fried calamari and a separate basket of French fries. Even though it was freezing and wet, the food tasted delicious, and I hardly acknowledged the elements at all.

After Ivar's, we made a rush to the hotel. We weren't sure if we wanted to go out for the rest of the night; it might be miserable outside. I watched a little television while Jim brushed the wet drops off his overcoat and shook off the rain from his leather hiking boots. We spent an hour in the room, and I took a look outside. The rain had stopped, and it seemed that the clouds were drifting away from the city. I suggested that we could go to the University District and break our ban on coffee shops. There were a couple of places I wanted to see; the first being The Café Allegro, a small, hip, artsy café that seemed cool, and the other being the University of Washington campus. Jim was agreeable, so we waited outside for the bus. The sun was almost gone when the bus slowly pulled up to the curb. There were about five people waiting, and a poor blind man was asking if this was the number three bus. Everyone ignored him as we shuffled into the bus and the blind man was left standing at the curb with the bus exhaust coating him.

The bus was pretty crowded, but quiet. The drive itself was not memorable, and with the darkness coming on, it was pretty hard to discern what the route was. Jim sat two rows in front of me near the back, and I was at the next to last row behind him. I just stared out the window with a blank mind, still feeling a bit tired and sleepy. The bus stopped off a block before the campus, and most of the people got off there. Must have been a lot of students on board. Our first task was to find The Café Allegro. We almost got lost looking for the damn place, and when I looked in my guidebook, it indeed said that the coffee house was very hard to find as it was in a nook near the campus. We did find another café though, Espresso Roma. It was a part-yuppie, part-student hangout that was quite popular. Local art hung on the cement walls and I ordered a large cappuccino while Jim got a large coffee black. We bought some newspapers and magazines at the rack near the entrance and hung out. It wasn't too happening, so we finished up our drinks and headed back out on our quest to find The Café Allegro. We almost got lost again, and I almost lost my temper with Jim. He kept on telling me he knew where the place was, but at every turn, it wasn't there. We finally happened upon it when we had given up and headed toward the campus. There, behind a bicycle shop, it was. It was small, with about four tables, and each table was occupied. We decided to pass and go to the campus.

I took a picture of Jim standing behind the entrance sign to the University of Washington, and then we strolled on the empty wet sidewalks that led past the physics department, the math department and finally we reached Huskies Stadium. It was huge. Though dark, we could make out the rows upon rows of seats on three tiers that must have been forty to fifty feet high, and you could make out the markings on the field below. There was a large, blue electronic sign that flashed the sporting events in yellow lettering and we saw the entrances to the locker rooms. A couple of campus security guards donning yellow windbreakers and carrying flashlights nodded to us as they passed by and we walked on until we left the campus. It was almost midnight by then, and we caught the last bus that would take us back to the hotel.

It didn't take long for Jim to fall asleep when we got back to the hotel, but it took me some time. Fishbone was playing at the Moore Theater, and you could hear the music echoing out into the street. The music stopped playing around one o'clock, and my eyes finally closed. Then, about fifteen minutes later, a hot rod decided to drag race down the street and I woke up. I looked over at Jim and he was snoring. I wanted to throw my pillow at him, but decided against it. I put my head down on the pillow and finally did get to sleep. For about two hours.

Day 3

The alarm shrieked with a vengeance at five. I opened my eyes, but they refused to stay open. I was dead tired and felt like crap. Jim groaned and rolled over in his bed. I willed myself to fall out of bed and knocked my head on the nightstand. That hurt. But at least I was awake. I stood up and pulled off Jim's covers. He swore at me and threw his pillow at me. I told him we had fifteen minutes to get out of the place. We hastily packed and changed. We went back down to the lobby. I dropped off the key and asked where we could pick up the bus to the airport. The raggedy white-haired receptionist pointed straight out the doors and said goodbye. It was a little chilly, but not wet. The bus came by ten minutes later and we hopped on. The bus was empty except for one person who was sleeping on the back seat. For each stop, more and more people got on. The strange thing was that they were all black people. One guy sat next to me. He had a newspaper under his arm, a black lunchbox in one hand, and a cup of coffee in the other. He nodded to me and proceeded to read the paper. Poor Jim was cramped up between three rather large fellows in the back. The closer we got out of downtown, more and more of the passengers were getting off. By the time we reached

I-5, there was only Jim, me, and the guy sleeping in back. We got to the airport at six, and our flight was for six-thirty. We jogged to the terminal, and I sat down as soon as we got there. I put my hand into my jacket pocket and felt nothing. I checked my inside pocket and it was empty as well. The tickets were missing! Jim was getting frantic as the plane was boarding the passengers. After emptying almost all of my backpack, I found them stuck in between my journal pages. Jim snatched his ticket from my hand and we hurriedly got on. We left Seattle and headed for home.

Author's Note- Coincidentally, on that Friday that we left Seattle, it was later known to Jim and I that Kurt Cobain, lead singer of the band Nirvana, had apparently committed suicide. It was on a last eerie note that Jim and I were there in Seattle when he killed himself.

Bus To Texas

It's almost midnight. My mom pulls the truck up to the curb, and I get out. It is still warm and muggy this September evening. I get my gray and black backpack from the trunk, and also a small, duct-taped box. My sister Erin carries my red daypack. We walk past the passed-out drunk still clutching the green-tinted bottle in his grubby left hand. A police car slowly drives by on the street. Newspaper pages drift on and off the sidewalk. The glass doors to the bus station are a welcome sight, and we all hurriedly go inside.

I go to the check-in, and the desk person tells me that the seats aren't assigned. You just show up and wait in line, and then it's first come, first served. There are a couple of lines that start across the other side of the brightly lit, fairly clean station. The first line is the one I am supposed to go to, so we go to the end of it. I drop my heavy pack to the ground, and put the box right next to it. My sister puts my daypack against the box. We stand there silently, not saying much. Everything that needed to be said was said earlier. Now is the time for me to start my journey. Erin says it's midnight. My bus leaves at twelve-thirty. The lines start right in front of a few clear double doors. Outside, there are slanted parking spaces for the buses. I have to go to the bathroom so I go across the station floor and up ten steps to the bathroom entrance. There is a yellow pyramid sign that reads, 'Wet Floor'. It isn't really wet, so the sign must have been there for a while. In fact, the floor is covered in grime. The bathroom itself is also not very clean. The sinks are filthy, the waste cans are full to the brim, and the mirrors are either cracked or non-existent. I try not to stay longer than I have to.

When I get back to the line, there are a few people behind my mom and sister. An elderly couple with and elderly lady are standing right behind us. The elderly lady strikes up a conversation with me. I tell her I'm going to Texas. She tells me she is headed to Louisiana. She keeps on commenting that I look like a Southern boy. I find that quite amusing, as I am Japanese. She says that I will surely love Southern hospitality. I hope so.

A bus parks in the space that is directly in front of our line, and I know I will be leaving on it soon. The front door of the silver vehicle opens, and about twenty people come out. They walk into the bus station, and people that were waiting inside greet some of them. The bus driver, wearing a light blue shirt and navy pants with a dark blue cap on his head, steps off the bus and disappears somewhere outside. My mom tells me that she and my sister should be leaving, as it is getting late and perhaps unsafe outside. I give them both a long hug and tell them I love them. I watch them walk through the station and out the doors. The PA goes on and a clear male voice announces that our bus will be boarding soon. A couple of minutes later, a new bus driver opens the doors that lead to my bus. He starts checking tickets and the passengers put their luggage in the storage compartment under the bus. He is quick and efficient as the line moves fast. I hand him my ticket, he takes his half, and gives me my half. Then I put my backpack and box in the storage compartment. I hop up the three steps that lead onto the bus and look for an empty seat. I find a seat next to the window on the left side of the bus, about halfway down, and I sit. I put my daypack in the vacant seat next to me. I sigh deeply, knowing I will not be in Texas until Tuesday afternoon. It's early Monday morning now.

The bus drives silently on the quiet, lighted freeway. I can hear plenty of Spanish on the bus, so I am guessing there are a lot of Mexican people with me. There is a problem with the air conditioning, so it is a bit warm. A few people shout from the back that it's too hot. I chuckle to myself and try to get some sleep.

We've stopped. It's a rest stop. I'm too tired to get off the bus, so I stay on. There isn't much to see; it's too dark. I can only make out the lighted truck stop sign nearby. A few people get off to buy food or drinks. I close my eyes and drift back to sleep.

I awaken and hear some voices. Apparently there is something wrong with the bus's engine. Great. I try to go back to sleep, but most of the passengers are restless. Some are asking what is wrong; most are chattering in Spanish. A baby cries out, and then starts bawling. I sigh and close my eyes, even though I know I won't be able to sleep. Half an hour later the bus starts moving again. I look at my watch, and it's almost five in the morning. The sun hasn't come up yet. I am hoping that the bus will arrive before six. My connecting bus leaves Los Angeles at six-thirty.

The light pokes through my eyelids, and I am instantly awake. I can make out the skyscrapers that is downtown L.A., and I know that the bus is close to the bus station. We drive through a rundown area of the city; where, I don't really know. Then the bus drives into the bus station, and parks in its slanted parking space. All of us shuffle out of the bus like zombies, off to our own destinations. I get my luggage from under the bus, and enter the station. This is a much nicer station; very clean and very busy. There are numerous people sitting and waiting for their buses. I find the information desk and ask where the bus to Fort Worth is. He is a kind, elderly gentleman and he points out the way. I sluggishly drag my luggage and myself to the line. There are already quite a few people in line. My mind is working very slowly, and my body is weary from the off and on sleep from the previous bus ride. I actually fall asleep for a few minutes in line, and the announcement that my bus is boarding startles me awake. A rather large, muscular man in uniform is standing next to the doors. He takes the passenger's tickets and moves the line. It is the same procedure; hand ticket to man, receive half of ticket, put luggage in storage compartment, board the bus. I get on and sit at a window seat on the right side of the bus, about three rows from the front. I put my daypack under the seat in front of me and relax until it is time for this leg of the journey.

It is a full bus, but I am lucky enough to have an empty seat next to me. The driver tells the passengers that this is the 'slow' bus, not the express bus. That means that the bus will be stopping at various stops along the way, and the final destination will be New York City. I sit back and look out the window. The bus starts to move and I watch as we go out of the station parking lot, and onto the street. There is some traffic, as the workday has started. We move past double-parked cement mixers. Shining, brand new BMWs and Mercedes speed in and out of the chaotic mix of delivery trucks, SUVs and other working class cars. The streetlights fade out, and the traffic lights blink green, yellow, and red.

The first two stops, Riverside and San Bernardino, are short and quick. In fact, it seems that they are just a part of incorporated Los Angeles. A few more passengers get on and one of them decides to sit next to me. He has a shaved head and has a mustache. He is wearing a white t-shirt and has a pair of faded blue jeans on. In his arms is a small cardboard box. He nods his head at me and I do the same.

The bus doesn't leave San Bernardino immediately. There seems to be a giant traffic jam on the freeway we are supposed to be on, so the bus driver decides to wait it out. There is a McDonald's nearby, and some of the passengers get off for breakfast. I decide to strike up a conversation with the guy. He is actually quite friendly. Animated and talkative, Jorge tells me he just got out of prison. Chino. Five years. For what, he never tells me and I don't ask. The box holds all of his possessions. He has a hand comb and he nervously combs the top of his head, his mustache. After fifteen minutes, the bus driver decides that he will try the freeway. The bus lumbers onto the street and takes Highway 10 East. Jorge tells me how he would wire his cell so he could watch television. Summers are the worst, he tells me. That's because they have no air conditioning and sometimes you don't even get to sleep. I ask him how he survived the time there. He says that by just being yourself. I shudder to think how it would be in there.

The bus gets onto Highway 10 unscathed, and we actually make excellent time to our next stop, Palm Springs. I never liked Palm Springs. And I was only in the city once before. Rude people there are, in Palm Springs. We pull into a tiny parking lot, and there is a door with the Greyhound emblem on it. A couple of women dressed up in L.A. Lakers cheerleader's outfits come aboard. Jorge says something to the effect that anyone gets on the bus nowadays. I chuckle.

Indio is the next stop, and as we drive on the baking asphalt and through a pass in the mountains, Jorge is getting anxious. His family will be waiting for him at the bus station. I watch the dead, dry bushes slowly sway in the scorching sun. The dirt seems to penetrate the air ducts of the bus and filter into it. A straight shot of three miles, and we arrive in Indio. Jorge grips my hand and offers me good luck. As he walks out of the bus, his mother, sisters, and girlfriend mob him. At least someone is going home.

I also meet some of the other bus passengers that had either boarded at L.A. with me or got on during the course of the ride.

Abdul is a cartoonist. Well, he is more of a drawer than a cartoonist, but he tells me emphatically that he is a cartoonist. He has a large drawing pad and he leafs through it showing me his original drawings. He and his grandmother are going to Mobile, Alabama to visit relatives. He sits in the front with his grandma.

Katie is seventeen. She has just dropped out of high school in Los Angeles and is going back to Texas where her mom lives in Weatherford. She is a kind girl with pulled-back blonde hair and blue eyes. She tells me that she wants to be a model someday. She sits across from me.

After Blythe, it is into unknown territory for me. I have never been to Arizona, but as we cross into it, the famed cacti are the first to greet us. Tall, green and thorny, I am imagining in my mind how it was like in the Old West, just riding your horse and wearing a bandana to cover from the dust. The heat reads over 105 degrees Fahrenheit. The landscape is dotted with the cacti, endless desert and in the far distance, a mountainous area. No sand dunes like Death Valley, though.

Three hours later, and we arrive in Phoenix. Whoa, is it hot outside! There is a change of drivers, so we have to disembark into the bus station. The heat is terrific, and if it weren't for the overhead sprinklers spraying cool mist into the air, we would have all melted, flying broom or not.

The bus station is crowded with people waiting for their transfers, and I go to the food counter to buy some chips and a couple of ice cold bottles of Snapple lemonade. Mmmm, it is delicious to fill my mouth and swim my tongue in the tart yellow liquid. I strike up a conversation with an elderly couple who is going to an Arizona Cardinals game. They are meeting up with their son there, who works in Tucson.

We board the bus after half an hour. The new driver is wearing a blue dress shirt and a navy blue tie. He takes our tickets and most everyone who is going on takes the same seats. There is a fellow driver hitchhiking his way back to El Paso. At this point I am getting a little weary, but it is still good to be traveling again.

We drive through the southern half of Arizona. As we drive into the interior, there is a spectacular desert sunset, with the silhouettes of the cactus in front of the mountains. The sun glows an orange-red and it is one of the highlights of the bus trip.

Tucson, Benson and Willcox are the places we stop in Arizona. The moon is full and bright in the cooling evening. The stops are uneventful; more passengers getting off and on. I sleep most of the time, and when I'm not, I stare out into the dark and try to see the landscape.

We arrive in Lordsburg, New Mexico around ten-thirty. We stop right next to the border of the USA and Mexico. We park right at the border station, and a couple of border patrol officers board the bus, asking for our identifications. Curt and quick, they exit the bus as professionally as they entered. But before we are able to leave, one of the officers re-boards and asks us who owns a certain backpack. Everyone is quiet. He asks again, and an African-American woman stands up. She has long, stringy black hair and she

115

is as thin as a rail. The officer ushers her off the bus and the rest of us twiddle our thumbs, impatiently waiting to get the heck out of here. About ten minutes go by and the woman gets back on. Later it was understood that the backpack was singled out by one of the dogs; the ones that sniff for drugs. If she ever had anything, I never found out.

El Paso. What an experience. We drop in at one-thirty in the morning. I feel like a stunned rattlesnake. We are to have another driver change. The bus station itself is very clean, and it has a few shops. I buy a tasteless Sprite and some candy bars. I sit next to an old Mexican woman, and watch the English-dubbed movie on the television. I almost fall asleep when the call to re-board is announced on the PA system. I drag myself back onboard and the new driver is a thin Mexican man who doesn't smile. He tears out of the parking lot and most of us passengers end up a seat to the left. Again I am blessed with an empty seat next to me. I take off my shoes, recline the chair and snooze the rest of the night.

When I wake to my first day in Texas, I see lots and lots of yellow grass. And in these grassy lands are grasshoppers. No, not the insect, but the oil pumps. There are what seems to be hundreds of them spread out all over the place. Up, down, up down. Pumping the black gold from the innards of the earth. This is all I see for the longest time, until we pull into Abilene.

Abilene, to me, seems like the perfect Old West town. The streets are empty, the heat is high and tumbleweeds DO roll across the ground. When we pull into the parking lot at Abilene, it is like going into a time warp. There is a Coke bottle vending machine, the stoplights hang from wires and the parking lot is filled with T-birds. Amazing.

The new bus driver is a giant of man. He is at least six feet tall and three feet wide, from front to back. His blue shirt barely fits him and I am sure that the buttons would fly off the shirt. He mumbles that it is time to go, and we all board one last time.

Cisco, Eastland, Mineral Wells, Weatherford (bye Katie), and then Fort Worth. The skyline is thick with skyscrapers and there is traffic. The bus wades through it and my final destination is here. I grab my bags and hope to start my new life here.

Will's Christmas Present

The night always seemed a little darker this time of year. The air bit with the cold of winter. Will exhaled the last of his cigarette and flicked it into the night. He felt pretty good about himself, knowing that he would get his Christmas present in a few hours. A car went by, and the lights flashed upon him. The white of his scalp was evident. The tight white T-shirt wrapped around his muscular frame. And the faint, yet prominent black swastika imbedded in his left arm faded into obscurity as the car passed by.

It was Tom's first holiday season. He had just finished his first semester at Stanford, and had passed all his classes with A's. He could vividly remember that only eight months ago he was boarding a flight from his native China. He had never been away from his family and this was the first time he had ever flown in an airplane. As he arrived to America to start his new life, he couldn't help but feel the pain he had leaving home. He blended in quickly as his host family took him in with open arms. He adapted to the lifestyle that everyone else took for granted. He ate three times a day, had a roof over his head, and always managed to have money in his pockets. He studied really hard; trying to get the grades needed to progress in his academic career. And now he made it through his first year in America. He was quite proud of himself. He felt as if he were an American himself. But every time he spoke, or every time he looked into the mirror, he was reminded of his heritage. But that didn't really matter. There was every kind of race here. And he fit in.

Will slammed the door shut of his Ford Mustang and revved up the engine. He gripped the wheel tightly and let the clutch go. The car spun around in circles, the air stinking of burnt rubber. As the car flailed around, Will screamed and shouted with glee. He straightened out the wheel and sped out of the empty parking lot. The blinking lights flashed off of the glossy red paint of the car. The lampposts were adorned with those fake Douglas fir trees. Even the faint sounds of sugary Christmas music could be heard. But all Will heard now was the hardcore epithets of Anthrax screaming into his ears.

Tom had just finished saying goodbye to his English professor and started to drive home. He had done all of his Christmas shopping and it was his first experience dealing with holiday shoppers. He had a rough time trying to pick out what he wanted to get for his foster family, but Emily helped out quite nicely. Emily was the first to greet Tom as he walked up their brick path that led to the two story white and blue trim house. She even stood there with the door open holding a specially baked cake that read, 'Welcome to America', on it. She had just graduated from Stanford and was to be Tom's guide and companion until he was situated in America. Tom chuckled as he remembered his first time on a computer and how he crashed it with just a click of a button. Or the time he and Emily went to meet her friends and one of them asked him if he ever ate anything besides fried rice. The drive home was not as bad as Tom had thought and he arrived home just in time for dinner.

Will banged the door to the liquor store against the outer wall and marched in, intent on his mission. He grabbed a twelve pack of Bud and a handful of Twinkies. A couple packs of Marlboros and he was done. He threw his money at the Indian cashier with a hateful stare and jumped into the car. He had one more stop before it was time. He drove a short distance and passed by a white and blue trim house. He stared angrily at it for the whole time he passed it, and then looked forward. He turned right and pulled into the driveway of a small yellow and brown house. The paint was worn thin and there were some holes in the garage door. Will went into the house and slammed the door shut. The living room stank of stale beer and smoke. The green carpet was stained with yellow spots and in more than one place it looked as if a fire had broken out on it. An older, balding man sat in a burgundy reclining chair, a cigarette pursed in his lips and a bottle of beer firmly grasped in his right hand. An evening talk show blabbed on the television. The man paid no heed to Will's entrance. Will went into his bedroom and looked for the final piece to his future actions. He looked on his unkempt bed and found nothing. A quick peek under the bed and he only found a copy of Nazi Monthly there. Then he struck gold as he found what he was looking for- a pair of nunchaku made of bamboo. He put them into his back pocket and glanced around his room for one last time. He knew that the next place he would be sleeping might be a room that had iron bars. The Nazi flag so prominently draped across his wall, a picture of Hitler against the other wall and the slogan, 'Whites Only', painted above his desk gave him a slight chill down his spine. He walked out, and the man mumbled something about shutting the door to the house. Will scowled slightly, started to pull the nunchaku out of his back pocket, but kept on walking out.

The dinner was something of a feast and Tom was delighted to see so much food on the table. There was a roast goose, mashed potatoes, yams, white rice, plenty of soda, and even some tea for him. The Watsons were always thoughtful of Tom's needs and wants. Though they weren't rich, they tried to give the best they could to their children. And now Tom was one of them. They all sat at the table eating and talking. It felt really enjoyable for Tom. He mentioned that he would like to stay another year and everyone was happy to hear that. After the meal, they all sat down next to the Christmas tree and listened to Christmas carols next to a warm fire. They ate some popcorn and drank eggnog. Tom sat back in his place on the couch and closed his eyes. He smiled and thought of how this was the greatest gift he could ever receive. His thoughts also wandered to home and he was sad to know his family was back in China working hard, so he could still go to school here. He loved them deeply and promised himself that one day he would give them the same experience he was going through now.

Will parked the car across the street, right next to the open lot. He turned off the engine and shut off the lights. The streets were poorly-lit, and Will knew nobody would see him at all. He lit a cigarette and pulled a long drag from it. The windows started to fog up a bit, so he cracked open a window. He turned on the tape deck and listened to Iron Maiden play through the speakers. Will finished the cigarette and started to punch the wheel in tune with the music. He started to punch faster and faster until the song stopped and his hands hurt. Before the next song started, he opened a beer and drank it down in one gulp. The music started again. After three more songs, three bottles of empty beer lay on the floor. Half a pack of cigarettes was smoked and Will was feeling good. He thought about how this was a tradition in his family. Now it was his turn to get his due. He remembered when his granddaddy lived in the South and how once he and a couple of buddies beat the shit out of a nigger. They tied him up to a tree and proceeded to beat him with baseball bats. Then they stripped him naked and threw honey and ants on him. His granddaddy could still hear the screams. Then his thoughts went to his own dad. Will looked at his arm and saw four old burn scars on his forearm. For the last four years, these were his Christmas presents. Will drank two more beers and put his head back on the seat. Now it was time for my own Christmas present, he thought.

Tom got up and said goodnight. He walked slowly up the stairs and went to bed. His last thoughts before he drifted to sleep were how good he felt and that everything was perfect.

The sun started to slowly rise. The light woke up Will with a start. He squinted a bit, and then threw a blanket over his head. Then, knowing he had to stay awake, he opened the last beer and drank it quickly. He smoked one more cigarette. Then he got out of the car and stretched. It was almost time. Will wasn't sure if he was going to get a chance, but inside his heart he thought he would. He took the nunchaku out of his back pocket and swung them around. The neighborhood was quiet, as it should be on Christmas morning. Will kneeled behind the Mustang and peered towards the house's front window, hoping to catch a glimpse of anyone who may be leaving the house. He waited for twenty minutes, but nobody was visible.

Emily came running in to Tom's room, rousting him out of bed. She wanted Tom to really experience Christmas morning early. Tom opened his eyes and saw Emily standing there. Her long blonde hair was tied back and she was wearing her pink nightgown. Tom smiled and got up. He put on his glasses and yawned. Everyone is waiting downstairs for you, Emily said. Tom nodded and they both ran down the stairs hand in hand. They opened presents and listened to Bing Crosby crooning out Christmas songs. As they got halfway through with the presents, Tom realized that he had forgotten Emily's present. It was in the back seat of his car.

Will watched his breath form in the air, anxious for any sign of that Chink to come out of the house. It was Christmas after all, and he may not show up outside. Will opened the door to the car and unwrapped a Twinkie. He mashed the whole thing in his mouth. The cream spewed all over his face. He wiped his face with his hand and glanced at the house. The door was opening! He scrambled across the street as if he were hunting an enemy. Out came the nunchaku, and Will knelt on the ground, hidden behind a pair of bushes. Then he saw him. The sun reflected off his glasses for an instant, and he was waving to someone in the house. The door shut and Tom made his way down the brick walkway. He opened the door to his Buick and as he bent over to reach for Emily's present BAM! A sharp pain shot through his head. BAM! Another blow hit his left shoulder. He heard a snap, and Tom fell to the ground. Will stood over Tom, smirking. You fucking Chink. Who do you think you are, huh? You don't belong here. Will raised the nunchaku, and as Tom raised his hands to block the blow, BAM! The short wood stick slammed into his ribs. Blood trickled from Tom's scalp and his glasses had fallen off. Will started to chuckle. This was too easy, he said to himself. Will raised his foot, and savagely kicked Tom in the groin. That's one for my granddaddy. Will rose his foot again to kick. It hit hard against Tom's broken shoulder. Tom screamed and rolled on his side. All he could think at this moment was the pain he felt all over his body. Yeah, Chink, it hurts, doesn't it? You motherfucking immigrant. You don't belong here. Wham! The nunchaku sticks hit Tom in the head again. Tom lost consciousness. Will spat on Tom's broken body and started to walk away. He made it to the Mustang when he saw the door to the house open. Emily ran to the driveway and saw Tom lying in a pool of blood. She screamed aloud, and then her parents came out. Will smirked and nodded his head. I got my Christmas present. He turned on the engine and sped off.

It took six months for Tom to heal, amid the broken bones, loss of blood and emotional scars that resulted from that fateful and brutal attack on Christmas Day. He read in a newspaper about the incident, and that they had captured a guy named Will Peterson, a known white supremacist and troublemaker. Will was arrested that day on a charge of robbery at a local liquor store. Tom also remembered that when he saw his attacker on television, all he could say was," I got my Christmas present! I got my Christmas present!"

Wave Riding

Chris came to pick me up. It was a chilly September morning. The sun hadn't come up and I was miserably tired. A sharp bang against my window startled me to complete attention. I perked my head off the comfortable pillow and didn't hear anything for a minute. So I put my head back down and closed my eyes. Then another bang against the window hit, and then another and another. I groaned and got out of bed. I looked at the clock: 5:30. The sun wasn't even up yet. I shuffled out of my room and went out the sliding glass door that led out to the backyard. I opened the wooden back gate and Chris walked in. He was dressed warmly in a red surf logo sweatshirt and a pair of dark blue sweatpants. On his feet he wore a pair of leather sandals. Hurry up, he told me. He was a bit irritated, probably because he had to get up earlier than me to get ready and pick me up. I mumbled something about the sun not being up yet. Chris motioned to the packed bags and yellow boogie board that waited under the metallic veranda with a sharp point of his left index finger. I went back inside quickly, knowing that Chris meant business, and I changed hastily into warmer apparel. Then I locked the sliding glass door, gathered my equipment, and loaded up into Chris's red Volkswagen Rabbit. He turned on the engine, and as the reggae music of Bob Marley resounded throughout the car's speakers, we were off to Highway 17 South.

Now, the road that is called Highway 17 should have been called The Snake. The reason being is that road, though paved and marked, was as windy and wily as a snake. The road went left to right to left again in a matter of seconds. On top of that, it went up, down and all around as the highway went through the Santa Cruz Mountains. Though the ride through the mountains was beautiful, I remember more than once clinching tightly to the chicken handle above me as the car would first weave towards the embankment, and then abruptly go towards the guardrail that protected us (albeit a weak one) from a tremendous fall into forest and God knows what else. But this ride through the mountain pass was uneventful as my eyelids hung just above my eyes. Sleep was beckoning its sweet solace, and the only reason I wasn't asleep was because the car would slice around a notorious curve and the tires would squeal against the friction of the asphalt. As we exited the mountains, the sun started its daily ascent into the sky. We had arrived in Santa Cruz safely and in good health. Now we just had to find a place to go surfing.

Chris had gone surfing before and he was more knowledgeable in the surf spots than I was. So it was up to him to pick a suitable place to ride the waves. Chris decided that we should try a place called Little Steamers. It was a break that was on the right side of a cliff. On that cliff was the Santa Cruz Lighthouse. On the other side of the cliff were the famed peaks of Steamer Lane, a world famous surf spot that attracted the best wave riders on the planet. We drove through an empty town. The traffic lights were all green and not a single soul stirred. I think the only place that was open was the Dunkin' Donuts. We got to the road that led us to the lighthouse, and I could detect the strong odor of the ocean- that pungent salty air that smelled like dead fish and salt water. We cruised by a couple of rusty old vans with surf racks and we actually saw a couple of surfers dressing into their black wetsuits and getting ready to go into the water. A guy waved at us as he trotted toward the stairs that led down to the water. We finally made it to the lighthouse parking lot, and there was only one other car. It was a green Volkswagen Bug with, of course, surf racks on top of it. Chris pulled into a space and we walked to the left of the cliff. That was where Steamer Lane was. The waves rolled in from about a hundred yards out and curved their way into the cliff side. Chris told me it was about head high. Not bad for a fall swell. In two months they would double in size. The waves came in and the crest would break right in the middle and there would be ample room for a wave face to ride on. A light wind chilled the air and the sky was a purplish orange; the sun's rays blocked and filtered through the dense fog and clouds. The lighthouse was in front of us, the beacon beaming its light into the sea. It was about thirty feet tall and whitewashed. The glass that reflected the light out seemed very clean. Chris rubbed his hands together and suggested we take a look at Little Steamers. We walked to the other side of the cliff and looked below. Little Steamers was alive and well. Its waves were the complete opposite of its older brother. The waves would come in off a rock known as Seal Rock, and slam into the cliff face. Then the wave made from the rebound off the cliff face connected with the original wave that was heading to shore. What it ended up being was a steep, A-framed wave that produced short, yet fast and hollow waves. A sure left that could hypothetically let you go all the way to the small strip of sand. I was quite excited and I was starting to shake. We went back to the car and changed.

Putting on a wetsuit is easier said than done. A one-piece suit made of rubber, with a zipper in the back to keep out the water and other foreign objects, is what it is essentially. First, to achieve maximum warmth, you should strip down into your own birthday suit. This is done because the direct contact of skin to neoprene keeps insulation at a maximum. With a towel tied around your waist, you put in one leg, and then the other. Of course your legs won't just slide through to the opening at the bottom. They'll actually get caught on the dry rubber about halfway down, and then you have to inch the rubber up each leg, while trying to keep your towel on, until you struggle to get each foot out. Then you can lift the rest of the suit with relative ease up to your waist and discard the towel. Then the same ritual happens again when you do each arm. But it's a lot harder because you don't have a couple of other arms to help guide the rubber up your arms. It feels like someone has put a strait jacket on you and you are immobilized. Finally, when the battle is over, and you get your hands to squirm out of the tiny openings, you reach at an ungodly angle behind you to find the tether that is attached to your zipper. You pull it up, (I bet you'll wince at least once), and the suit is on. It feels like wearing ten sets of clothing all at once. You feel stiff, you can't bend at the joints too well, and when you walk, you look like an oversized penguin waddling on the sidewalk. I won't even describe to you the putting on the wetsuit socks either. The only other gear you need is a pair of swim fins and your board. The swim fins are short and specially made for boogie boarding. Their purpose is to give you exploding acceleration when kicking. A little wax on the board for grip, and then it was off to the beach.

The sidewalk led to a couple of flights of wooden steps, and we waddled our way as fast as we could go down them. At the bottom there was a small beach and you could see that the faces of the cliffs around us were made of sandstone. The beach was completely empty except for some piles of kelp that must have come in when the tide did. Chris sat down and stretched his hamstrings. I did likewise. Then he put on his fins, as did I. Then we both stood there for a few moments to wait for the set of waves to end. A set of waves usually consisted of four or five waves that came in succession of each other. And then there would be a lull. We waited for a couple of minutes, and then our lull came. We exploded off the beach, if one could do that wearing fins and carrying a boogie board under your arm, and right before the water hit the shore, we jumped into the ocean. The first thing you will feel is complete shock, as at around 55 degrees, the water is quite cold. The cold doesn't just hit at your exposed head; it permeates your entire body. It is a feeling like standing out of the shower when it is wintertime. That cold. Then, after getting over the shock of that frigid water, you paddle like hell out towards the ocean before that next set starts. Chris, the more experienced one, made it out before the next set arrived. I, however, was not that fortunate. As I floundered on my board, trying to maintain balance, I was in the impact zone. This is where all the waves broke. Chris frantically waved me to get out where he was, but I couldn't accelerate fast enough to make it past the incoming waves. I could see the sets forming, but I had no chance. The first wave broke over my head with vicious strength. The wave caught me and threw me over itself, rolling me under the water. My board slipped out from under me and I rolled over and over and over. It was like being on the spin cycle in a washing machine. Then, as I opened my eyes, I saw the churning of the water above me and my body twisted this way and that way. The wave finally let go and I desperately kicked for the surface. With a deep inhale I took in some much needed air. And then the next wave pummeled me. It wasn't as strong as the first one, but it essentially took me all the way back to the shore. I got up exhausted and sat down. I saw Chris pointing at me and laughing. Ha-ha, I said to myself sarcastically. I didn't want to go back in.

I sat and watched Chris catch some waves. He would turn his board and start paddling like mad towards the shore. As the wave crested, he would go up the face, and eventually come down it, as his momentum of going forward would propel him onto the wave. He would hold the right side of his board and tilt his body towards the face. The wave was breaking behind him with great speed, but he managed to keep just ahead of it. Then the wave would catch up and engulf him. I laughed silently to myself, as I knew what his fate would come to. But miraculously he would appear back onto the face of the wave, and then turn out. There were other tricks he would do too. He could go onto the face of the wave and make his board do a complete circle. All he did was add weight to one side of the board and the speed would turn the board around, either clockwise or counter-clockwise. And the most spectacular feat of all was when he would catch a wave, gain maximum speed by doing a turn at the bottom of the wave, and angle the board to the crest. The board and Chris would fly up over the wave and hang in midair for a few brief seconds until he came back down, either on the face of the wave or where the whitewater rumbled about after the wave broke. Filled with this excitement, I wanted to go for another try.

I sat and studied the ocean. I tried to get in tune with the vibes and feelings of this dangerous beast. I watched each set come in, counted the timing of each wave where it broke, and how long it was. After fifteen minutes, I felt confident enough to try another go at it. I waited for my lull, and then rushed onto the water. I paddled like a psychopath, arms flailing all about, legs and fins splashing water all around me. I made it out to Chris in record time without a hitch. As I wearily slowed to a stop next to him, he shook his head and smiled. Welcome to the party, he chuckled. The hard part was over, or so it seemed.

The next set started to come out. I watched Chris as he would maneuver himself to a spot on the water, and when the wave was right upon us, he would paddle with a tremendous ferocity towards the shore. Then the wave would engulf him and I wouldn't see him at all. I saw a wave I wanted to catch, so I tried. The first time I didn't paddle fast enough and the wave passed by me. The second time I paddled too far in and I looked in horror behind me as the jaws of the wave engulfed me. It was back into the spin cycle. I popped up like a cork and was lucky to not have gone too far from where I first started. On top of that, the wave I tried to catch was the last of the set. I paddled back and sighed with displeasure. Would I ever get to ride a wave?

The next set rolled in. Chris customarily caught the first one, and he did. I watched the wave into the shore and saw his board and body launch out of the water. He took it in all the way to the beach. I let the next two go by and decided that I would go on the fourth one. I got into position and paddled as hard as I could. I looked behind me and saw the wave forming. The wave took me up its face and I could see the foam rising on top of the crest. I paddled like I was paddling for my life and a tsunami wave was going to obliterate me. I was right at the top of the wave and just when I was about to give up paddling, the board slid down the face. I was on it! I turned my body to the left and the board went with it. It felt exhilarating! I couldn't hear anything, I couldn't think anything. I was just there. I looked at the glassy face of the wave next to me and saw a faint reflection of the sun. The water was clear; not the murky blue I was accustomed to seeing. I rode it all the way in and ended at the shore. Chris smiled and nodded his head. Welcome to the party, sir. I laughed and sat down next to him. My first wave. What a thrill.

Stevie-Boy

The helicopter started to leave. The blades rotated, and the wind generated by them made everything fly away. As the helicopter went up, my mom and dad saw Steve wave goodbye. I was only 6 months old, so I say this from what my mom told me. My mom took my hand and waved it. And then he was gone. To another country. To fight a war nobody wanted.

I'm 22 now. The sun was shining brightly. He came to the house around 10 am and I got up to say goodbye to my grandma. She waved and watched her Fox News intently. I grabbed my backpack and went out the door. Steve was waiting for me in the car. I got in and shook his hand. He pulled out of the driveway and we were headed north. He played slack guitar music on the tape player. I opened the window and felt the nice, warm, humid breeze on my face. By the way, my name is Steve too.

We made it to the north shore in about an hour. When you go there, you have to drive between the sugarcane and old pineapple crops that have been there for many, many years. When you start going downhill towards the north, you can see the ocean. Today was nice. The ocean looked a deep blue and the clouds were not visible. We drove into Haleiwa and saw the familiar sights that you see there. The shaved ice place that had a line going out the door. The surf shop with all the kids hanging out and trying to meet a famous surfer. The Foodland that was just built there a couple years ago. Here we would have to drive slowly. We went through the town and drove into the 7-11 driveway. We bought beef jerky and Slurpees.

Steve was a quiet man. But when I was with him, he was not quiet at all. With salt and pepper hair and a thin body, he was always nice to me. He was my mom's favorite cousin. Not only for his personality, but because they were close in age. Steve played the guitar. He had a studio in Aiea, where his parents still lived. He collected music magazines and was good to the family dog. But he had missed the best parts of his younger years because he got drafted and had to go to Vietnam. This experience changed him forever.

We drove to the northern most point of Oahu and got out. There were rough waves and coral. The wind was always a bit stronger here. But cooler. We looked out to sea and enjoyed the view. He asked me when I was going to move to Hawaii. I was non-committal. I told him hopefully soon. After resting there for half an hour, we got back into the car. We drove to a beach that we had always hiked when I was visiting. We went to the sand and there was nobody there. We walked and walked. Steve asked me if I was happy as a poet. I said yes. We looked at the million dollar beachfront houses, and he said that if I was lucky, maybe I could live in one of these houses and write. I smiled. The water touched my bare feet and the sand was very soft.

Steve was in Vietnam for four years. He was part of the pullout when we left the war. He told me of the mosquito bites he would get in the jungle. He told me of the latrines he had to clean and the countless potatoes he peeled while on KP duty. But he never told me what he did when he was on patrol with his unit. He never told me if he killed anyone or was in battle. The only thing I knew was that he was awarded the bronze star for valor.

We walked to the end of the beach and found ourselves at a river mouth. I hiked up my backpack as high as it would go on my back and put on my slippers. The water was waist high and you could feel the tide pulling at your body. We crossed without incident and reached the other side, where there was a small sandbar. We went up the small sand dune and walked on the crabgrass. There was a horse trail and we followed it until we reached a huge coral shelf. It was white and dry. And very sharp. We walked slowly and carefully down the shelf and reached another beach. We saw a couple of small islands out in the water. There was a golf course on the left. Steve said he was going to teach again, perhaps to students from the university, and maybe some high school kids. I remember listening to him play guitar with his brother when I was small and he was phenomenal. So talented.

Steve lived with his parents for his whole life. He had a good childhood and played with my mom, my aunt, and my other cousin. His brother. They would play football on the baking asphalt. They would play hide and seek in my grandparent's huge house. My grandma would take them to the beach in the summertime. When Steve came back from the war, he was not the same. He kept to himself. He was withdrawn. You could see the vacant eyes that always stared into nothingness. He was a changed man. But nobody ever figured out why. Of course, war changes people, but there was no record of what happened. There was no recollection of death. So we were all clueless. But we accepted Steve for who he was and let him be.

We went back to the beach where the car was. We dusted off the sand that clung to our lower legs and feet. Then we went back to Haleiwa and stopped by a pizza joint. We had cheese and pepperoni and a pitcher of Coke. We sat in silence and ate. Then we window-shopped at the clothing store next door.

I was happy to be with Steve. He always seemed so kind to me, and we were close for cousins. Even though there was a large age gap between us, we got along really well. We went to a liquor store and bought a six pack of Heineken. Then we went to a local beach and drank together. After a couple of hours sitting on the beach and drinking beer, we left. He took me home at 6 pm and I said my customary goodbye for the summer. I'll see you next summer my favorite cousin.

Call

And what do I say to her? I miss you? I love you? I want
you to be right here with me in my arms? No, of course not.
I will say, 'Happy Birthday', and make small talk and have
a meaningless conversation that will always end up as,
'Call you soon. Take care.' And then I will hang up the
phone and feel that deep twisting ache in my chest. My
eyes will water and warm my pale cheeks. And then I will
not call her again.

The first time I smelled her was on that Tuesday
afternoon in July. The window was open, the sun shining
in. It was a rare nice day. The light frothy breeze drifted
into the room, and it tangled into her auburn hair. It teased
and tickled, and finally when it passed, it danced to me, and
her scent absorbed into my face. It was a sweet, flowery
smell, a smell that I most often sniff when I walk by a red
rose bush. I closed my eyes and I thought of nothing else
but to be there, with her.

There was the time when I was with her, and she was
reading a book. She was so entranced by the book that her
brown eyes sparkled with interest and passion. I couldn't
take my own eyes off her. She suddenly glanced up and
caught me staring. But instead of looking down in shame or
shyness, I kept my gaze. I couldn't do anything else. I felt
paralyzed. And then I realized that I loved her.

It has been too long a time since I have seen her, and it makes me very sad to know that I am almost to the point where I forget what she looks like. But the feelings are still the same. My heart leaps when I hear her soft words on the telephone. I can feel her pillowy lips on mine when I think of those nights when we kissed under the London moonlight. And her warm hand in mine, so tight and secure as we would walk through the streets, not seeing anyone else, not hearing anything else, only seeing and hearing each other. I smile when I remember, but my heart cries.

The dial tone ticks away in its methodical sequence. Three times and the line goes quiet. 'Hello?' I say.

10.30.2000

Tomorrow I go home to San Jose. After almost eight weeks in Texas things haven't changed that much, if at all. I am more tired than I have ever been and my mind is soft and fragile. All I want to do is sit and watch television or sleep. My eyes have big black bags around them; the sparkle seems to fade in and out of the irises. I walk a lot slower; I feel exhausted. I feel like I am sixty years old. The dreams have gotten worse. I fear for my life, as the dreams have been nothing except death and suffering. I wonder if I am to die soon. Right now all I can think of is to go home and hopefully recover from this mysterious, yet soon-to-be deadly sickness that I have contracted. Well, it isn't like I haven't had this sickness before. It has been with me for quite some time now, so long that I almost can't remember when it first came into me. The grip of its poison is getting stronger and stronger with each day and I am starting to believe it may be time to get all my affairs in order.

Is it worth living if one has their life intact, yet does not have the tools or the passion to live their life to the fullest? People steal dreams from others all the time and even lives. But, my thoughts are, if I were to have a normal life where I wasn't being oppressed or tortured, would I be able to live a normal life? I won't be able to know, I fear.

The voices have been getting louder. Dead. Death. Gone. The words stab into my heart and soul. They twist and skewer like a bloodworm under my skin trying to get at the next blood vessel. The story is almost finished, and then it will be told to the entire world to learn and understand the tragedy that I have partook in these last few years. Unfortunately, my death will be the beginning of the end for them, and rightly so, as not one human being is worth more or less than the rest. Human existence in terms of personal lifetimes is adequately finite, but where the soul goes afterward is the truest form of one's existence, of their deepest faith and love and compassion, if they are capable of that in their human existence. Heaven and Hell seem so black and white, but it defines a lot. At almost thirty years old, I never would have thought my life would have come to this point and time. But it has, and to accept it as a mortal is not only faith in where I am going after I leave this world, but knowing that what I leave behind is even a greater and more wonderful thing than anything else, including my life in human existence. I have become tired of judgments from the basis of human ignorance and narrow-mindedness. We have such a long way to go. I feel like I am standing in the future trying to make people understand that the present is not the end. Nor is it the link to the past and perhaps a path to go there. The future of our humanity is in the future. Let us shed these violent and oppressive skins that we grasp onto so tightly for warmth. Is it the cold that we are so scared of? Or is it the fear of not knowing what would it feel like to not have them drape over our still-sloped shoulders of our ancestors of thousands of years ago? There are glimpses of the future. I can see them in between the spilled blood and lifeless bodies. A child smiling when a soldier gives them a flower. A helping hand to a man who can't stand up after falling.

Gift bringers and well-wishers to those less fortunate. That is only the tip of the iceberg. But are we so scared to see the rest of the iceberg? Or are we so selfish that we must protect our own self-interests to the point we will kill and oppress and lie and steal away other's lives and emotional possessions? I am a man who is almost broken because of the statement I just said. The worst thing a human can do to another is to rob them of their freedom to live as a human being, and to have the choices and the ability to make them. I don't know if the world is half-dark, or half-lit.

I go home hoping that I will be able to heal. I am not so sure that will be possible. The demons, which have been with me for so long, now, seem to keep their claws firmly sunk into my flesh. Their lies are hell-bent on destroying my human existence and me. I must not fail in my mission to make sure that when my soul leaves the temporary embodiment of transition, my message of peace, love and compassion will be left here for others to keep and use. And to finish the evil that lingers behind. Thank you God for giving me the life I have had to learn and understand. I know now.

Thoughts On Love

It was the end of the world. A shadow of sky hung heavily above. The wood worn planks of the skinny platform creaked under the constant motion of water going from sea to shore and back again. A breeze picked at the branches from the overgrown trees that grew from below. I saw the sun glow its bathing light against the strewn-about clouds, the rays danced red and orange. It seemed that the sun wanted to bring the clouds to wherever it was going to next, a companion to keep company on its perpetual journey of loneliness. Those memories from long lost arrived so eloquently on my soft mind. It was she again, and those times we spent so lovely and endless together. I saw her stand before me with her deep brown eyes full of curiosity and passion. The slight glint of playfulness flashing in and out in a heartbeat. I smiled to myself and wondered how she was doing. I missed her a lot. I waded my feet in the calm water and it felt warm, warm like her touch on my bare back. Her hands kneading at my tired and tight muscles. Or her soft kisses against my cheek when I woke up in the morning. I sighed and I felt that familiar twinge in my heart that always spoke true. Seemingly connected to my eyes, the warm salty drops formed and ran down my face. What did we talk about when I last saw her? Good byes, good lucks, I wish you well on your journey and your life. Don't ever forget me. A kiss. And then she left my life.

It was getting cold and the light of the sun disappeared. The stars started to appear. *Star light, star bright, first star I see tonight.* She used to say that every night as we looked out of the skylight. The deep blue turned into a darkness that only reflected the light of the stars and planets. *I wish I may, I wish I might.* She closed her eyes tightly as she recited the words, very child-like. *Make this wish I make tonight.* I wish you were here with me.

I lied back on that old wood pier and studied the stars. Was she looking at them at the same time as me? Maybe she was, maybe she wasn't. The moon was half-visible; it looked like a shadow of a giant white ball hanging effortlessly in the night sky. The last moon I remembered was when I lied on the floor. She lied next to me in her bed. I saw the moon's rays shine on her silky, creamy skin. Her full pouty lips were perfectly lined. The locks of her auburn hair were tousled above and beside her pillow. The rise and fall of her chest was slight and small. A serene, peaceful sleep. I stroked her face and smiled. My love for her was deep and forever. She moved and I stopped. I kissed her lightly, and then went back to sleep. My dreams were filled with soft ocean breezes and warm sunshine. The lapping ocean waves made me comfortable and happy.

It was time to go inside. I left the night and stars. But I never will forget her. I will always love her. I will always be there for her. I miss you. I love you. Forever.

Back To Seattle (And A Dash Of Canada)

Midnight has finally come, and the air is as cold as ice. We leave the restaurant and hop into the van. Jeff takes the wheel, while Mike sits shotgun. Paul and I lay out on the lounge chairs in the back. Jeff turns the key and the engine roars its angry voice into the darkness. The headlights pierce the night and Jeff pulls out of the parking lot. Gravel and rock fly from the squealing tires and we are off on our journey north.

Soft rock weasels its way onto the radio and I look out into the night, not quite drowsy yet. Paul is snoring peacefully across from me and Mike is also sleeping. Jeff, his grip tight on the steering wheel, seems to be driving by Braille as the van goes over the divider lines every so often; its duh-dump duh-dump duh-dump telling me that we aren't really driving straight. It's a little cold in the van, so I pull on my jacket. Jeff starts to hum to the music on the radio, and I try to get some sleep.

It has been five hours on the road and the only things keeping Jeff company are the passing cars and big rig trucks we keep on passing. The landscape is covered by the thick darkness, except for the odd road lamp. I wake up and wish instantly that there is a bathroom available. I tell Jeff to pull over to the next gas station. As soon as the van stops, Paul instantly awakens. He follows me into the bathroom. Mike is still asleep, his head lying against the window. After emptying my bladder, I grab a cup of black coffee. Jeff fills up the tank and Paul buys some mini-doughnuts.

146

Paul takes over driving duties and I rouse Mike, so I can take shotgun. Mike squeals with irritation and slowly moves behind me. Jeff, happy to get some sleep, relaxes back into the lounge chair and closes his eyes. Paul pulls out slowly from the gas station and we are off again on the asphalt jungle.

The sun barely peeks over the relatively short-peaked mountains in the east. The stars are just about gone, as the skies become lighter and lighter. We are almost out of California as dawn comes and goes in a few, but momentous minutes. Paul is a quiet driver, his eyes stuck on the road. I yawn and close my eyes, but I can't seem to go back to sleep. I fiddle with the radio and find a good classic rock station. Led Zeppelin's 'Stairway to Heaven' comes on just as we pass the gigantic, yet comatose ice covered Mount Shasta. On days like this you can see the mountain for countless miles.

We stop at Ashland, Oregon to fill up. Mike's a little grouchy, so we start calling him 'Oscar', and Jeff seems to be a bit spaced-out. Paul mentions that the Shakespeare Festival is going on, and that it is too bad that we aren't staying. Ashland is a small town that is filled with pines and mountains. It would be a nice place for a writer's retreat. We all get back into the van and head north once again.

All is still quiet except the radio. The landscape is plentiful with fir trees lining the highway and snowcapped mountains to the east of us. Paul looks into the rearview mirror and spots a jeep with two blonde girls driving right behind us. Paul lets up on the gas and signals them to the side of the road. Roadside picking up. We pull to the side of the road and waste time chattering to a couple of nice girls from Eugene. Then it's back on the asphalt for us as we part ways.

Fifteen hours, three states, and countless rantings and ravings from Oscar have taken a toll on all of us. But as we start our last descent into Seattle, it seems that everyone is in a good mood. Five in the afternoon and we hit gridlock. An hour later we arrive at The Ramada. We get a ninety-nine dollar a night with two double beds room. We only have half an hour before we are due at Sky City, the revolving restaurant at the top of the Space Needle. We all SSS (shit, shower, and shave) and hurriedly dress in ties and slacks. Mike and I are carrying bottles of cabernet sauvignon. This is my second foray into Seattle in three months. We drive to The Seattle Center and take the elevator up to the restaurant. We are immediately seated and get a great table right against the glass windows. The food is good, and the wine even better. The bartender comes over and gives us a sampling of some expensive cognac. Jeff, the alcohol snob, looks the part as he swishes the amber liquid around the clean snifter and sips from it liberally. As the restaurant rotates around, we get an amazing scene of downtown Seattle with the humongous Mount Rainier in the backdrop. The light is a soft violet and the skies start to darken. Mike plays note tag with a girl sitting behind us. I shake my head and quaff the rest of my wine. Paul, the great wine master, pours me another…and one for himself as well.

From my memory, I can't remember when I shared a bed with another man. Well, the last time I could recall was when I was a young boy and I would sleep on the pullout mattress with my snoring grandpa. I don't remember how long ago that was- twelve, fifteen years ago? Anyways, I was assigned with Mike in one bed while the burly men slept in the other. With Jeff screaming clucks out the third story window and Mike's farting games, I am at wit's end. Thank God the wine is working as one by one, everyone falls asleep. As with all my memories, I would cherish this moment. And Mike, no kisses or hugs.

I am the first to awake and it's very quiet except for the methodical snoring of Paul. I'm surprised that nobody else is awake. I get up, use the bathroom and brush my teeth. I turn on the television and watch some cartoons. Half an hour later Mike wakes up and starts his mumblings already. He stumbles into the bathroom and slams the door shut. Paul moans and rolls over as Jeff gets up and starts to comb his hair with his hand. We finally get out of the hotel by noon and we are going to go to Fremont, a part of Seattle near the University of Washington. We find this cool hole-in-the-wall called Land and Sea, and we each have a hot bowl of creamy clam chowder. Mike dips crackers into his steaming soup while Paul crumbles them into his bowl. We also order some sandwiches and wash everything down with soda. Then we go next door for the obligatory coffee from Starbucks. It's a small deal with a couple of tables and a nice coffee bar. I order a large cappuccino while Mike orders a café latte. Paul gets some funky Costa Rican ground and Jeff opts for a frappuccino. We go out into the

149

warm Seattle day and window shop at an odds and ends place that has T-shirts of old television series and dressed up mannequins. Paul takes a few pictures, and then we hop in the van and head towards the ocean.

Bainbridge Island is our next stop. Paul wants to see it, as do I, since I didn't go there from my earlier trip to the Northwest. We take a slow ferry to the island. There is a nice observation deck and you can see the boat pulling away from the city. The view is pleasant and picture worthy. The sun is shining brightly and there is a light offshore breeze. The smell of the sea is salty, but not pungent. Paul, Mike and Jeff explore the ferry while I just stare out into the ocean. After twenty minutes the ferry pulls up to the dock and we all meet back at the van. Jeff drives out of the ferry and onto a seemingly well-built road. Bainbridge is mostly a rural type of island; small on buildings, but great in charm. First we stop at the supermarket, and there are these bottles of wine that have a picture of Marilyn Monroe on them. Paul and Jeff buy a couple bottles each and I buy a six-pack of Guinness bottles. Then we head back onto the road. We go along, driving and seeing farms and houses that are right off the sides of the road. The island is quite small, so it only takes an hour to go around it. We end up at one of the docks and there is a small bookstore. We wander around the peaceful area and find a pub right on a dock. The place looks well-kept and the dock is full of tables and chairs. We decide to grab an early dinner and I order a huge helping of fish and chips and a pint of Guinness. Everyone else buys the same and we pick a table right on the waterfront. It feels like a lazy day in spring, with the boats rocking back and forth gently with the tide and the ocean breeze slowly drifting in and out. The place gets packed, but the same quiet, quaint atmosphere prevails and everyone gets to enjoy it. We toast to Paul's birthday and eat silently at the table. And then it's back to the city limits on the ferry, with the day almost at an end. We all watch the sun go down past the ocean's horizon, ready to party it up in Seattle.

We look and look and look, but we can't find a decent bar or pub. And none of us brought a guidebook. We slum the clean streets of Seattle for a good booze establishment, but we end up snake eyes. Just as we are about to end our beer hunting, we find a bar inside a hotel. MTV is blasting from a television set and there are only men in suits drinking at the bar and at the tables. I order a scotch and soda and the rest order beers. The scotch tastes good. My alcoholic self is in heavenly bliss. We all end up drunk off our asses and Mike hits on the waitress. She gives him her number and Mike says she might join us tomorrow on the next part of our journey. I think she has a fake English accent. But I later find out it is Australian. We hobble back to the hotel, and Paul and Mike want to hang out at the hotel bar, so Jeff and I go back up to the hotel room and crash. No playing around for tonight as Paul and Mike come in an hour later and silently slip into bed like a missing spouse.

Ten o'clock and I am the first one up again. Our next destination is Victoria, British Columbia. I try waking everyone else up, but all they do is moan and yell expletives. So I watch television until each of them get up and grumble and bitch about how early it is and that they didn't get enough sleep. We get out of the hotel and we don't stop for breakfast. We drive straight up the highway until we reach the border. There is a giant sign saying, 'Welcome to Canada', made from bushes and flowers. We stop at the booth. The immigration agent asks us if we have ever been to Canada before, and we say no. So we have to go into the office and fill out some papers while they search the van and our belongings. We almost get busted for the wine bought from Bainbridge the day before, but they let us off with a warning. We cross into Canada and drive for about fifteen minutes on Canadian soil until we turn left towards the ferry landing. There are long lines of trucks and cars waiting to load onto the ferries. We get to the pay station and dish out fifty bucks for a round-trip ticket. Then we drive onto the ferry parking deck and get out to look around. The ferry is huge. It consists of two decks, one for the cars, and one for the passengers. There is a duty-free store on board and I buy a Vancouver Sun newspaper. You can either sit inside or out on the deck. We ramble around and check out all parts of the accessible areas of the ferry. Paul takes some pictures. The ferry starts to pull out to the sea and starts the hour-long journey to Victoria.

The ferry ride is stunning. As the boat cuts through the dark waters, we pass islets covered in firs. The air is fresh and breezy; the sun feels good on the face. We end up sunbathing near the end of the ferry. There are plenty of people on the ferry as most are sitting on the sides of the ferry soaking in the sun or sitting inside reading a newspaper or drinking coffee. So everyone is relaxing or enjoying the free time while the ferry takes us to Victoria.

Sadly, the ferry ride comes to an end and we all get into the van. One by one the cars and trucks drive off the ferry and onto the asphalt. There is a sign that reads, 'Welcome to Victoria, B.C.' We follow the windy road that hugs the coastline. After half an hour we arrive in Victoria. It is a medium-sized city with an English feel to it. The most prominent sight is the Empress Hotel. It is an elegant, yet large hotel that looks very Victorian English and it has some beautiful portraits of kings and queens hanging in its venerable halls. They even have teatime right at four in the afternoon. The Empress faces the waterfront and there are sailing boats coming and going, or still moored on their docks. Then there is the Parliament. It looks almost exactly like the Houses of Parliament in London. The city really has an amazing English feel to it.

We decide to park the van and walk around. We find a small pub and order food and beers. Afterward Paul and Mike see a moped rental stall and they want to rent a couple of mopeds. Unfortunately I start to get stomach cramps, so I decide to take a nap near the waterfront. There are small patches of lawn to lounge on. Jeff decides to join me and we fall asleep in the warm drowsy day.

After Paul and Mike's forays into the inner parts of Victoria, we find a nice restaurant to eat dinner. My stomach is feeling better, so I order up. Beers flow freely around the table while the bar in the restaurant has a television set with a baseball game playing on it. Full and content, we head back to the van and drive back to the ferry landing. By the time we get there, the sun has gone down. The air has a slight chill to it, so we decide to stay inside the ferry. The ferry glides silently on the water, a full moon shines in the cloudless skies. I can't make out any of the islets we pass by, but I know they are there from the dark areas. We arrive back at mainland Canada and head back to Seattle. We manage to smuggle a few Cuban cigars past the customs agent on the US side and we drive fast to get back to the hotel before it gets too late.

We find a great club called Rock Candy. It's a bit dark inside, but the grunge band playing is pretty good and the girls are pretty. We all sit at a table on the second floor and hang out. After an hour, we head to the local twenty-four hour restaurant for pancakes and coffee. Then it's back to the hotel for a nip of sleep.

We get out of the hotel early as we have to drop Paul off at the airport. He has to work, so he has a booked flight at noon. We meet up with Mike's cousin Rain, a massage therapist. She is really nice and chatters away about her life in Seattle. We see Paul off at the airport, and then start the trek back home.

Jeff and Mike almost kill each other on the ride back, but we make it back in one piece. It was a good trip and a lot of fun. But next time I think we'll leave Oscar at home.

European Travel Journal 2001

Author's note- This travel journal has been minimally edited to keep the authenticity of the journal intact.

Day 1- 09/04

London. I've made it. Finally. More than eight years and countless fears and worries later, I gathered the courage and inspiration to come back to what I call my 'first real home'. It wasn't an easy road though. I had to find God to give me the strength and courage to go beyond my fears and worries, and I found Him, and His omnipotent existence was partly infused through my soul. Second, I had to personally overcome evil. As they say, The Devil comes in many forms, and in my case, it was fear, voices of darkness in my mind, and the threat of my life to end. That is why I had to find God again. I couldn't fight the battle alone, and I am forever grateful and dedicated to The Lord and His mission for me. That's why I am in London. The message was sent, and my soul responded. And now I am here. There was a harrowing two-day, two-flight trip starting at Honolulu, stopping over at Minneapolis-St. Paul and ending at the unfamiliar Gatwick Airport in England. I was pretty beat up emotionally and physically, but my mental state was clear and strong. I enjoyed the taxi ride (though not the fare) through London's southern suburbs, through London Proper at Chelsea and Battersea, and finally back to my own romping grounds of Bayswater. Again, I had brought too much luggage, and again, I had spent way too much for convenience's sake. But I was extremely excited and happy to be back. I almost wanted to kiss the many years' thick polluted coated asphalt. Almost.

As I closed my door to my hotel room, I sprang down the four floors worth of stairs, and felt like a new man. I felt energized, as if a great burden had lifted not only from my heart, but my soul. The sun was shining brightly and there was a cool breeze wafting through the air. People were walking on the sidewalks, and I smiled at each and every one of them, and if there was eye contact, I said hello. Some did return the greeting; most put their heads down and walked by. Things had changed a bit since I left. But the buildings still looked the same. The same pubs, the same newsagents, the same congested traffic on Queensway and Bayswater. They were all the same that I remembered. My first task was to go to a Fish and Chip shop and buy a large batter-covered piece of cod with fresh chips blanketed with vinegar and salt. It took me a while, but a place where I had bought fish and chips before was still there, and I got a really nice piece of cod. The chips were just cooked. It was double-wrapped in a gray wrapper, and the grease was already starting to soak into it. Then I went to a newsagent and bought The Sun tabloid newspaper, The Evening Standard newspaper, and Time Out London. And without paying the outrageous prices at home! A 1.5 liter of Coke was the last item I needed, and then I was on my final mission. Weaving through traffic and the sea of people coming towards me, I made my way down Queensway until it dead-ended into Bayswater Road. And there it was, flush against Bayswater Road on the opposite side. The place I had always loved and enjoyed walking in and through: Hyde Park.

I found an empty bench at the shore of the Serpentine, with gigantic white geese lying on the grass behind it, and sat down. The water was alive with waterfowl. Plenty more geese were gliding on the surface, along with a few swans dipping their slender necks under the water to cleanse themselves. Countless pigeons were fighting each other for the scant crumbs on the shore. I sat down, took a gigantic guzzle of Coke, and turned my face towards the sun. It felt good on my skin. Clouds were smeared against the baby blue sky, and they would intermittently drift in front of the sun. The breeze was more of a light wind, but it felt refreshing. I ate my fish and chips slowly, peeling the batter and grasping in my fingers white fleshy chunks of warm cod. I savored every chew; it was delightful. The chips were delicious as well. I read my papers and said hello to a few passersby. There wasn't anywhere else I wanted to be. There was only one tweak to this perfect picture: the voices were back. It always seems that when I am feeling good in my life, the voices have to steal that good feeling from me. 'You're dead'. 'We'll beat you'. 'It isn't over yet.' But, my heart didn't drop like it used to. Because God was sitting right next to me giving me strength and enjoying my experience with me.

In life, I have always been curious about everything in it. Whether it is what it means to be human, why we do what we do, or why we don't do what we don't do are the questions that always grate on my mind. I swear, I must think about it twenty-four hours a day. I have a firm grasp of Good and Evil, but I cannot relate or understand the mechanics, mentality or capacity of an evil human, an evil soul. Every time that I think I know the answers to Evil, I experience something that makes Evil even worse than I knew it as. How can humans destroy each other, when we can be capable of creating such beauty? Please, don't get me wrong, Evil isn't the only thing that exists. Good lives just as strongly as Evil, and I have experienced Good. In fact, I consider myself a Good person. I always wonder why I have to be surrounded by Evil? I guess only God can give me the answer to that when I die. But my only rational, logical guess is that God is testing me. To prove my faith, to prove my worth, to prove my goodness. With the gifts God has given me, am I being a worthy human being by helping others through the gifts I have been anointed with? Well, so far it has been a very difficult test. Satan is always poking to find holes in the armor, he is always trying to break you down and enter your soul and plant that seed of Evil inside. He whispers lies into your ears, and tries to destroy you with fear and confusion. But I know God is there for me, and it has helped me in my test. I am not afraid.

It is almost time for sleep, and I am going to see the place where Tiffany used to live up at Willesden Junction. I am sure my emotions will be very strong when I set foot there. And then I don't know what I'll do after that. Maybe call my friend Ben. We used to work together at a hotel. Those were fun times.

Day 2

A day of reflection. A day of memories. A day of tears and sadness, and of fondness and love. I awoke early for this journey I had been anticipating for the longest time.

Remember when, in your life, how good you felt in certain times, when everything seemed so new and fresh, and that time didn't matter. When you knew in your heart that THIS time in my life is the most beautiful and perfect of my life, and I may perhaps never have a time like this ever? When I went to London in the summer of 1993, I met the love of my life. I still look back and wonder how it all happened, but sometimes there aren't answers to some questions. Sometimes there are just feelings and thoughts. And harmony with another person that will never occur with anyone else in the world for all time. Tiffany Silverman was the most intriguing woman I had ever met. She was a quiet, unassuming girl who wore a baseball cap and dressed in blue jeans and rolled up long sleeved shirts. But she had these deep brown eyes that just saw right through me. The first time I looked into her eyes, I had a twist in my gut that I hadn't ever felt before. My heart would start to race and my mind was stunned. I couldn't be around her too long before I would have to excuse myself. As our time together progressed, we became great friends, and in my heart, she became the love of my life. The more I was around her the more I wanted to learn about her. I couldn't have enough time with her. In a small room in a flat at Willesden Junction, we shared secrets, looked into each other's eyes, played games. We enjoyed each other's minds, hearts, and bodies. I felt so free, so light. She could always lift any dark cloud from over me. There are countless other things I loved her for, but I am going to be selfish and keep them to myself. But it would take many, many pages to list them all. This was the time that was the most beautiful and perfect in my life. Now, eight years removed, I was finally ready to remember, to smile and to cry.

The sun was trying to peek through the thick gray clouds, but there weren't any cracks for the light to shine through. I brushed my teeth and changed my clothes. My face was starting to peel from the sunburn I received in Hawaii, and I picked off flakes of skin. After a half hour of doting with my face, I loaded my backpack and headed out. I checked my email and made a couple of calls to Valencia, Spain to find out the availability of hotel rooms. Then with a slight spring to my step, I ventured out of the hostel ready to meet long lost memories.

I did a few errands first. I bought a plug adapter for my laptop, changed more money, and bought some water and a newspaper. Then it was a few hundred yards to Bayswater tube station, and I bought a four zone all day travel card. The tube! I hadn't been on it for eight years as well. But the scene was still the same. The same maps, the same steps leading down to the tracks, the same trains clicking and clacking on the tracks, and the same hair-raising screeching of the train brakes that seemed to reach every inner ear. Lucky me, the train just pulled up. I had to go one stop to Paddington (Circle Line) and then transfer to another line (Bakerloo) that would take me to Willesden Junction.

Paddington was a station that was a crossroads for a few other tube lines therefore that was why it was so busy. I walked with authority through the crowds of people going to their own destinations. Unbelievably, I didn't get lost. I guess instinct does work its mysterious powers. The waiting area was in a tunnel with a thin concrete platform. Chairs lined the wall, and there were a few vending machines scattered here and there. The platform was mostly empty, except a couple that were waiting with me for the train. Five minutes in that enclosed stuffy tunnel was almost too much for me. But the wind from the train took away the stifling heat and I got on a section that had only one other person in it. I felt the familiar rhythm of the train go back and forth as it sped forward on the electric tracks. I stared blankly through the window, my mind was placid but also thinking about the times when I would ride this very tube line to go see Tiffany. I sighed and felt my eyes water.

The ride took about fifteen minutes. It was uneventful except for the stark scenery that the train passed by. I saw graffiti-covered buildings, run-down, abandoned trains on solitary tracks with weeds growing at least five feet high. There were black, soot-stained brick homes with some broken windows. The skies were still gray and non-luminous. And then Willesden Junction stop finally came. I had to step up onto the platform and avoid a large pile of dog excrement. I took a second to take a look around. It hadn't changed much from what I remembered. It still looked old and tired, dirty and sad. But for me, I felt a bit of warmth in my stomach. I was back.

I took the walk slowly. The neighborhood still looked and
felt the same. Though I don't remember all of the buildings
that I saw when I was here eight years ago, most seemed
renovated or clean. The same tract of houses I walked past
were still the same; each and every house coated white and
the curbs lined with cars on each side from the beginning of
the street to the end of it. When I emerged to the main
street, I knew where I was. I was probably only a couple
hundred yards from Tiffany's old place. I walked east
towards the main intersection. The air was crisp and cool. I
browsed at the buildings I passed by while I walked. I saw
the Chinese take-out shop we used to patronize, and I took
a couple pictures. Then I walked across the street and saw a
sign that read 'Furness Road'. I headed down Furness
Road, and saw the old familiar places that were still there.
On the right, the Mom and Pop Italian ice cream shop was
still there, the same with the off-license store next to it. On
my side of the street, there was the same Arab-owned
grocery store. The inside looked a bit different as I passed
it, but it was still the same store. The old telephone booth
that Tiffany used to call home was still in the same spot,
but it looked like it had been replaced with a newer model.
The primary school was still there across the street, and as I
got closer to Tiff's old flat, I used the school as a marker to
where her flat would be. We used to wake up in the
morning to the school children playing on the playground.
Then, there it was. 26 Furness Road. The white washed
door looked run-down. There was garbage scattered on the
ground. The black and white tiled floor was still there, but
someone had piled some of the loose tiles in a corner. I

wanted to go inside to see the place where I had the best time of my life, but nobody answered the door when I knocked on it.

Honestly, I felt kind of numb. It was like going on a tour of my past life. Just being a tourist to my own past. The feeling was quite different this time, and I attributed it to not having shared the experience with Tiffany. But the more and more I walked around the area I felt the flood of memories come into my mind's eye. I remembered the walk to the grocery store with her. The walks to the Laundromat under the semi-sunny skies. Sitting on the porch under the star blinding night, talking and sharing. The sadness started to sink in and I made a few more walks around the neighborhood before I knew in my heart it was time to go.

I wonder what will happen in my life. Will Tiffany and I ever have what we did those days so long ago? Or maybe that was it, and I have to hold on and cherish them? I understand that life goes on, but for myself, I feel like I am without half of my soul. I will leave it up to God as to the outcome of my life. But I will always love Tiffany the same from the first day I loved her to the day I die. *I knew I loved you before I met you.*

Day 3

I awoke on this day and felt a little dirty. Oh yes, I hadn't taken a shower since I left Minneapolis and it was two days later. Yuck. I took a nice leisurely shower, and enjoyed the hot water washing my body. It was refreshing and invigorating. My face was peeling profusely by now, and it looked, as one guy said, 'like you just got scalded by boiling water.' Yikes. My shoulders were starting to peel as well, and I was taking off bits of brown skin like peeling the candy off a fruit roll up. No matter. I changed into shorts and a t-shirt and re-packed my backpack. Today was the day to foray into the heart of the concrete jungle.

I had never visited the British Museum. My thinking at the time when I was living in London was that I would be here for a while so I would see it whenever I wanted to. Well, I never made it to the British Museum. And there I was, rocking back and forth again on the orange Central Line, headed to Tottenham Court Road tube station. It was a quick ride, and as I exited the station, I realized that I didn't know where the museum was. I thought perhaps it would be in close proximity with plenty of signs showing the way there. Never saw the signs, and I took my own route. And that turned out to be the wrong one. Well, on a scale of 1 to 10, 1 being barely lost, and 10 being completely and utterly lost, I was probably a 3. Panic didn't set in like it used to when I got lost, and I took the liberty of asking storeowners if they knew. I only lost probably fifteen minutes, and finally down a small alley did I see the British Museum. It was a block-long Roman monstrosity, with giant columns lined in front of the entrance. Above the columns were statues covered in gold leaf, and there were a lot of people. People sitting on the steps that led to the entrance, people milling around like pigeons pecking for food, people walking in and out of the museum itself. I made my way to the entrance and bought a small guide to the museum. The entry to the museum itself was free. I went in like a happy schoolboy just let out of school, and I took a left up a few flights of stairs that led to the early English/Roman history rooms.

The artifacts were astounding. There were ancient swords that were in rusted pieces in showcases, various pots and items used in everyday ancient English/Roman/Celtic chores, and many, many symbolic stones that had carved icons of the worshipped deity of the times. It was sensory overload. In fact, I saw so much in the museum that I had to take pictures (which I normally don't do) to have memories of what I saw. I did get to see what I really want to see: The Rosetta Stone. It took me two times to see though. The first time I went there to see it, there was a German tour group blocking the stone and its case. So I came back later and then it was partially blocked by a Japanese tour group. But I edged my way in and saw the most important artifact found in Egypt. I was stunned to see that this piece of rock was a translating piece of work that unraveled the ancient hieroglyphic language of the Egyptian pharaohs. There was a woman feverishly jotting down notes on my right, and it seemed that there were a few other scholar-type people looking the obsidian rock up and down and also taking notes for research. Amazing.

The rest of the museum that I saw was varied and glancing. I saw some ancient Chinese artifacts and also Korean and Japanese. There was also a pay-to-get-in gallery called Shinto. It was a gallery of ancient artifacts and pictures dating back in the 1300's of feudal Japan. There were samurai swords, wooden carvings of Japanese people, and also paintings that were stories of ancient gods and the world of the time. For myself, being a Japanese-American, it was a wonderful diversion from the rest of the hustle and bustle of the main museum. I also saw the African part of the museum, with fertility carvings and ancient African tribal shields donning the display cases. There was the Near Eastern room with all of the stonewall carvings of the Indian culture, and also the Middle Eastern room with ancient Islamic texts and artifacts. To name everything I saw, and mostly what I didn't see would be impossible without a two or three week everyday visit to the museum. Yes, it is that huge.

After getting sensory overload from the museum, I was going to go to another landmark of London, though this place was not one of your check-and-see-then-go types of places. I took the same tube line a couple stops down to St. Paul.

When you leave the tube station at St. Paul, there are numerous signs that tell you where you are and what you are looking for. I found my own destination and followed the easy-to-follow arrows that led me to St. Paul's courtyard. The courtyard itself is spread around the whole cathedral. There are grassy knolls and a path cuts its way around the cathedral like a moat. Plenty of people sitting on wooden benches eat their lunch or read pensively. It would be a nice place to get away from the hustle and bustle of London. I walked around the whole circumference of the cathedral and took in the breathtaking architecture of

Christopher Wren. Not very easy to describe, but as it's commonly known to Christians, it is a conduit to God himself. I found the front entrance and walked up the marble steps and into what would be one of the most spiritual experiences I have had so far in my lifetime. It was cool and quiet, and the soothing hues of amber and red would put any troubled soul at instant ease. The cathedral was, in one word, huge. The ceiling was infinitely high, and the columns towered from above. What struck me most was that though I saw many people in the church, it was nicely quiet. I walked into the main cathedral and sat down. I closed my eyes and felt warmth throughout my body. I felt at home and at ease. I said a small prayer of thanks to God, and then I walked to the dome section of the cathedral. I saw some frescoes of something, but I couldn't make them out. So I decided to take a better look, up to the place called The Whispering Gallery.

There are 259 steps that lead to The Whispering Gallery. The stairs are made of wood, and the spiraling staircase goes from right to left. This is not a recommended climb for those who aren't in good shape. I didn't rest at all on my way up, and I paid for it when I did reach the top. I was sweating profusely and my shoulders ached from the strain of my backpack. But, an overwhelming calm flowed through me. I looked up at the frescoes, and I could see, in my eyes, something simply divine. Though hard to describe, it reminded me of the Sistine Chapel and the frescoes painted on its domes and walls. The paints were a soft brown, and gigantic god-like figures were floating in the skies. Below the frescoes was a circle of statues that

167

were saints. There were eight total and they were spread out evenly around the dome. I looked down below and saw the cathedral's floor. It was teeming with people. I also saw the massive organ that piped its melodic music throughout the cavernous halls. It had tall, black pipes that reached up high. I wish I could have heard them sound off.

From the Whispering Gallery, there is another flight of 119 steps to the Stone Gallery. It goes to the outer part of the dome, and there are some spectacular sights of the city from its circular vantage points. These steps were made of white stone and the halls were so narrow, even I had a close encounter with them. I wondered how someone bigger than me could get through, though skinny Horshack could probably go through easily. It was cooler and a bit windy up there, but what a sight! There was a wondrous sight of the Thames, its murky brown waters flowing towards the English Channel. The view above the concrete jungle gave me a sense of being above the chaos that us humans have created for ourselves. Why? Who knows? But it was better being up here than down there.

For those who just have to see the whole package, there is the dizzying last gasp climb to The Golden Gallery. 152 steps from The Stone Gallery, it is the highest point that can be reached by any mere mortal on St. Paul's. That's a total of 530 steps from the base of St. Paul's to the Golden Gallery. The stairs that wind up the cathedral to The Golden Gallery are painted black metal and narrowly wind upwards. This was probably the worst flight of steps out of the three. I did have to stop two times to catch my breath.

When I walked through the tiny stone opening, the sun was shining through gray London clouds and the view was even more wonderful. The walk-around took less than a minute, and the path was two feet wide, if that. Only one person at a time could walk, and none could pass them. I took a few pictures and then headed back down. It was a wonderful, spiritual experience to be here.

When I got to the bottom again, I looked closer to the further parts of the cathedral, like the South Quire Aisle and the Apse. I passed by the pulpit, which had a microphone attached to its top, and I also saw the choir stalls on my left as I walked through the South Quire Aisle. The Apse held a memorial dedicated to the American soldiers who fought in World War 2. Then it was time to go below the chapel, and into Europe's largest crypt.

Massive marble statues and busts adorned the hallowed halls of the crypt. Most of the tributes were for heroes of war, like the Duke of Wellington and Lord Admiral Nelson. They both had impressive monuments. There also was Florence Nightingale, William Blake and Henry Moore. And tucked in a little corner of the farthest part of the crypt was the most gifted of architects, Christopher Wren. His stone crypt was black and quite simple. The attendant who helped me find his final resting place told me of Christopher Wren's wish not to have an extravagant crypt for him. A true humble servant of God, the cathedral of St. Paul and the countless other churches he built was his legacy. He did not need an extravagant grave.

I went for a quick look at the London Treasury, which held the various treasures from London churches, ranging from silver and gold crosses to bright chalices and elegant priest's robes. Then it was time to go.

Day 4

Rest day. My legs weren't particularly helpful in getting me to walk. I could feel the deep tensions in my quadriceps and hamstrings, and they were also sending out dull pain signals to my brain. Well, I said to myself, perhaps I really am getting old. So I decided to rest this day. It wasn't that I had to do everything at once, see everything at once. I wasn't on a planned itinerary, and in fact, I was probably more into just being in London than seeing it. Being in London for me was to see, smell, touch, feel, and hear the city moving and shaking on its foundations, watching the behemoth live and breath like any other. I had more insight by walking the streets than going to see the tourist attractions. Also, I had lived here for six months already, and the city, to me, hadn't changed much in my eight-year absence. It still felt like the same vibrant, enjoyable city I had known before, and the only thing that really made me sad was that I was exposed to more negative-minded people than before. But in all walks of life, in all civilizations, there are those who are like that, and I use 'negative-minded' as a kind gesture, for I am not a human that judges or criticizes my fellow humans. But one cannot help but feel the urges of judgment on oneself. It must be an instinctual thing. But, even with them, it hasn't changed my view of London or the people who reside in it as well. I have been going to a newsagent for the last three days. He is a middle-aged, Indian man who is probably only a couple inches shorter than I and has a graying mustache. He always greets me hello as I buy my beverages and newspapers. We have a good repertoire as customer and storeowner, but it goes past that I believe. There is a sincere friendliness between both of us, and thank God there is still that. I also met this 24 year-old girl named Kate. She is from Poland and she has been working at the hotel I am staying in for about four months. She is 4'10, has medium length blonde hair, and a pair of black-rimmed glasses that highlight her dark brown eyes. She is a nice person and I enjoy saying hello to her every time I see her at the reception desk. The world isn't so bad if you look for the good in it.

So, the whole day I did nothing. I sat on my bed, listened to music, watched movies on my computer, and ate. I did venture out in the late afternoon, and I bought my newspaper, bought my water, and took out some cash from the ATM. I guess I do have a routine of sorts now, and it is good to get out of my cramped room for at least a while. I went back and then read my newspapers, drank my water, listened to more music, and played a computer game. I enjoyed the day relaxing in my London. I probably will do the same on Saturday, as the places I want to see will be quite crowded. I still have a hard time dealing with tourists. My belief is that you really don't get to know the real soul of the city if you just visit the obligatory tourist attractions and pop into a pub for a quick pint. No, you have to see the city from the ground level. That's probably why I won't go to the Eye of London, basically because of tourist reasons. But I still would like to see Trafalgar Square, Piccadilly Circus, Buckingham Palace and St. James Park, and Earl's Court. These places hold more memories than anything else, and I will hopefully get to see all of them in the last two days of my stay here in my old home.

Day 5

Another day of slacking off. I must be getting old and dry if I am so inclined to stay in my room for two days straight. I think I am just waiting for Monday to come so I can get on the plane to Valencia and see new places, meet new people and learn a new culture. Maybe I am already bored with London. I don't know. But I guess once you have been somewhere once, the second time around isn't as exciting or wonderful. Don't get me wrong, my time here has been fun and I have enjoyed being here. But when you have lived in the place for six months, and you come back, it's to reminisce and remember more than living it again. Especially since I am only here for a week. The funniest thing is that when I first made my mind to go to London, I only planned to stay for three days. I thought that three days would be enough to see all the old places I remembered and been to, and that also I didn't want to waste a lot of time and money in a place I already knew. And yes, London is still quite expensive if not more expensive since I left and came back. Let's see. I think when I was here in 1993, the 1-2 zone all day ticket was around 2 pounds and 70 pence. Today, it is four pounds. The newspaper prices have stayed the same, and also the food I have been eating, which has been a mixture of rotisserie chicken, fish and chips (for the food snob it would be 'cod and chips with vinegar and salt') and jacket potatoes. Lovely, those jacket potatoes. They are basically baked potatoes that have heaps of condiments placed in the split middle. My choices have always been sweet baked beans and cheese. My friend Tarik, whom I used to work with at the hotel, was the person who introduced me to them. At the time, they were perfect. Easy on the pocket and fulfilling to the stomach. Even now when I eat them I am in heaven. Trust me, try them, you'll love them. Anyways, back to the cost comparison. Well, perhaps I am wrong in the fact the London has gotten more expensive. I think only the accommodation (single room for forty dollars a night) and the tube tickets are the only significant mark ups from 1993 to now.

When I do stay in, I usually will go out to get my newspapers, water and whatever I am craving to eat at the moment. I go to the same newsagent, and I go to the same take-outs. When I get back to the hotel, I will open the window and sit there on a stool reading my newspapers and eating my food. Most of the time it has been cloudy, but today was a cheerful bright, and there was even a semi-warm wind. The streets echo their sounds up to my window, and I can hear kids screaming, police sirens wailing and cars screeching down the pavement. It is life in London.

Day 6

This is my last full day in London, and even though the day
isn't over, I will write what I have done today. I awoke
early, around six-thirty in the morning. I wanted to get an
early start to see the last places I had on my itinerary. The
sun was barely up, and the swath of white clouds painted
the skies. I took a quick shower and packed my bag. I was
off to downtown London again, but more into the touristy
areas. I walked down the quiet streets, the air was crisp and
cool, and it didn't have that legendary London pollution
mixing in. I went on the Circle Line East to Embankment.
That was the stop I would get off at when I was working at
the camping store Alpine Sports on The Strand. When I
exited the station, I saw the same narrow street that was
lined with various eateries. The Dunkin Doughnuts shop
was gone, sadly. There were a few new places, like a wine
bar and a hotel (!), but the feeling was still the same as if I
were going to work again. Fifty yards uphill, and the street
opened onto The Strand. The Strand is the more popular of
the shopping streets in London. It was surprisingly not
crowded, but it shouldn't have been as it was eight in the
morning on a Sunday. I walked west down The Strand for a
hundred feet or so and took a street north that led to
Trafalgar Square. There was the same bench I ate lunch on.
This time there were only a few pigeons grasping the top of
the bench with their claws. A few people were milling
about, feeding the other pigeons or just sitting on the other
niches reading newspapers and sipping coffee. The sun was
just climbing into the sky and it shone right through the
spray of the twin fountains. It was quite beautiful. Lord

Nelson was still perched high on his pedestal, and the fierce lions were on each side of the pedestal. I remembered the picture Tiffany had taken of me sitting in front of the right lion. We got ice cream at a vendor that was right in front of the lion statues. St. Martin's cathedral was still magnificent as always, and the other buildings I was accustomed to seeing everyday were still as tall and strong as ever. I bid haste from the area and headed to Westminster Abbey and Big Ben.

My walk was a pleasant, quiet one. Not too many people at all, and the brisk autumn weather was my dream of what London would be like at this time of year. I followed The Thames from the north side, and I saw the 'eyesore' as the locals call it here. The Eye of London is more like it. But I was not interested in riding a super-sized version of a Ferris wheel. Leave it to the tourists. Hahaha. I finally stumbled upon Big Ben, but I was a little disoriented as I was expecting to see it on the corner I was about to walk to. It was across the street. I guess I have forgotten a bit of London after all. I took a couple of pictures of the splendid timepiece, and I also took a few pictures of the Abbey. It was closed, and I wasn't about to go inside again. I already knew what was there. Long live Henry V!

I followed the sidewalk that surrounded the Abbey, in hopes of finding St. James Park and ultimately Buckingham Palace. I, of course had to get lost at least once in London and so I did when I went this way instead of that way. I think I walked around in a two- mile circle as I found myself back at Big Ben. I stopped at the tourist kiosk and asked the man if he knew where it was. He laughed and said he had no idea. But he let me use a map and as he looked over my shoulder trying to help me, I looked up and there on a giant white sign were the exact directions to St. James Park. We both looked at each other sheepishly and I thanked him for his time.

The walk was now getting a little tiresome. My legs were getting weary and the crowds were starting to thicken. I looked at my watch and it was nearly nine-thirty. I found the park right away, but I didn't know where the Palace was. I saw a police van parked on the street and I hoped to get directions. Of course there wasn't anyone in it or in the close vicinity, so I winged it and tried my luck by going to the right. I walked a bit until I saw a crowd of people standing around what looked like a curved barrier in front of an elegant looking building. I looked on an enclosed board map and it was the soldier's quarters. In fact, as I found the directions and started to walk in that direction, there was about twelve men or so dressed in red military dress riding white horses on the street, lead by a policewoman. The Queen's guard, perhaps?

The walk to Buckingham Palace was not too eventful. My feet started to hurt and I could feel a blister starting to form on the ball of my left foot. The windy stone path cut through the deep green grasses. There were people here and there. I ran into some aggressive geese and I was sure to get poked. But they were more interested in the young boy and his family as they tossed out pieces of white bread. Then, I saw the tri-posts painted in gold leaf stabbing into the sky.

Yes, I was at the entrance of Buckingham Palace. I walked up a flight of steps, and the park opened into this gigantic open area. There were a few statues, and the tri-posts were lined around the perimeter of the area. And, in all its glory, Buckingham Palace was right smack in the middle of it. To tell you the truth, (and I can hear you readers sighing and shaking your heads) it wasn't the same sight for me. It was not unspectacular, but it wasn't spectacular. I took some pictures for austerity. There were plenty of people though. Almost too many for me to deal with. So I didn't stay. I walked back towards the other side of St. James Park and headed for the hotel. Well, sort of.

My plan was to walk all the way from Embankment station to Bayswater. Of course, it sounds better than it looks. And in the course of trying to get back to Bayswater, I got lost. Yes, I got lost. I think it is a prerequisite for me when I am in London. No matter how much I think I know the streets of London, no matter how much I know about the directions I give myself to get from one place to the other in London, I get lost. As so I did. For the next hour or so I spent walking around SW1 and went this way, went that way and anyway but up or down. My legs were starting to give out on me. I was getting thirsty as well. And after bumbling around for that hour, I saw a sign for Victoria Station. Which only told me I was walking pretty much in circles instead of getting to Bayswater. With a humiliating feeling in my gut, I got onto the tube and went back.

Famished and thirsty, I bought a jacket potato and a rotisserie chicken from Hart's Grocer. Then I bought some water and three newspapers (Sunday Mirror, News of the World and Sunday People) from the same newsagent I had been buying my papers and water from. I told him I was leaving tomorrow and he wished me good luck. I felt a little sad that I wasn't staying here, but I think my mind was ready for a new adventure. And, I think I missed doing this with Tiffany. But life goes on. And so do I, to Spain.

Post script – I did receive an email from Tiff this morning, and I was actually quite skeptical that she would write back. I don't know, but I had this gut feeling that she wasn't going to write back. But she did. She wants to come here and visit like I did. She is supposed to meet me in Paris. Hmmm, I wonder how that will turn out. Eight years without London, and now eight years without Tiffany. I try not to think about it as I embark on the next destination.

Day 7

My time in London complete, it was time to leave my favorite place in all the world (so far) and time to move onward. I packed too much and I suffered as it took me almost a half-hour to get to the tube station that was only a couple hundred yards away. Stop and go. Stop and go. That is what I did to make it there. I vowed that this time I would not travel this way again. The tube took me on an uneventful ride to Heathrow Airport and I checked in at Iberia Airlines. At 4:20 my plane would be leaving for Valencia, Spain. I doted around for two hours, doing nothing and waiting for my gate to appear. Yes, I didn't have a gate assignment even two hours before departure. So I ended up checking the departures monitor and it finally showed me at 3:45 that it was Gate 2. I casually walked to the gate and felt freer than ever before. I was entering new territory, a new country, and a new culture. I had always liked Spanish culture, and I took six years of Spanish language in high school and college. As the plane left the airport I was very tired and very thirsty. I hadn't eaten anything and my body ached from the carrying of the bags. I looked forlornly out the window and watched London disappear as we lifted into the clouds.

The flight attendants were quite friendly. They offered beverages and food with a smile and seemed very confident and tight knit. The airplane was quite modern, and every three rows there was a small television monitor that had the news, commercials and tidbits of the airline. Very bright and comfortable, this was a change from my usual experience with US airlines and their services. We even got a full dinner and the flight was only two hours. I sat next to a couple from Valencia and I held my own as we discussed Valencia, the football club and Spain in Spanish. I felt confident and excited to be using my 'other' language and to be conversing with a Spaniard. The flight went quickly and we touched down fifteen minutes early in Valencia airport. With a hop in my step and my heart beating excitedly, I stepped onto Spanish soil for the first time in my life.

I caught a taxi to the city center, which was about three miles away. The first thing I felt when I exited the airport was the humidity and heat. Wow, what a change from cold, cloudy London. It was as if I were in Hawaii again. The taxi driver was quite friendly and we bantered about the city and its landmarks, food and history. Again, my Spanish was used and I felt more and more confident using it. But I could tell that I was still rusty, as I would forget the odd correct pronoun or mispronounce a name or three. But the driver was quite forgiving and he would smile or ignore my mistakes. Then I had this vision in my head that said, 'I wonder if he is laughing at me inside'. I, too, laughed inside and watched the city pass by. My feelings about the city seemed very intrigued. Most of the buildings were quite old and there were even some structures that were made probably many hundred years ago. But the night was coming and it was harder to identify the various structures.

I arrived at my 'hostal' and I paid the taxi driver for the ride and his company. Finally here in Valencia, I got my room and stowed my bags in my room. I was thirsty and I wanted some water.

I took a short stroll down Plaza del Mercado, and the street was like a neighborhood street in any European city. There was a small café that had all kinds of beverages, a tiny pharmacy that had your basic drugstore items, and a few small shops here and there. Most were closed though, as stores would close before nine in the evening. I found a telephone to call home, and then I went back to the café to buy some cold bottled water. There were two things I was well aware of that I needed to work on: how much and where. How much, meaning the cost of things and making sure I wasn't paying more than I was supposed to. Also, looking for discreet markups that the travel books said that was in practice. So far I wasn't short changed, but I was beginning to observe and see. In a different culture and speaking a different language, it is easy to trick the unknowing tourist out of his or her money. My direction sense has always been quite good, but again, with the language being different, street signs can be very hard to decipher. Luckily I asked around when I didn't know where to go, and I always had a small map from the travel book I was using. I had to buy a more precise one. As I finally crawled to bed, and another weary day's travel behind me, I stripped naked and lay on my bed in the dark. As I was starting to finally drift off, a loud, babbling baby running up and down the outer hallway kept me awake for the next hour. Aye, aye, aye.

Day 8

Oh the pain! That was the first thing that entered my mind as I awoke fairly early on this Tuesday morning. My body was stiff from head to toe and I was in agony. I slowly got up and tried to stand up. Yow! My left foot was burning with pain, as the popped blister was still raw. I hobbled to the mirror and took a look. My God you look a mess. I went to the toilet and then lay back down on my bed. It was getting warm and muggy and I was starting to sweat profusely. I wasn't very happy. In fact, I was downright irate. I stayed on the bed for about an hour and decided that I should get up and take a shower. So I took a nice shower and got all cleaned up. I changed and went down to the reception desk. I asked if I could get a single room instead of the double I was staying in. There still weren't any available. This place was going to cost me too much for a three week stay. I had to find another place. I left the hostal and walked about a hundred feet to another one. It was half as much and I was pleased. Famished, I started to look for the Mercado Central, or Food Market. On my way there I saw a small display of postcards and decided to buy a couple. As I handed them to the shopkeeper, we proceeded to have a nice conversation about Valencia and the people. He told me he was from the Dominican Republic and that it was paradise. I could tell that he wanted to go back. After a few minutes I bade him goodbye and headed for the Mercado. There, above the gigantic open doorway was a sign that read 'Mercado Central'.

It was a giant, indoor market that had numerous stalls selling fruits, vegetables, meats, cheeses, and fresh bread. It was lovely. It reminded me of the markets down in Honolulu, when my grandpa would take my sisters and me each Saturday to buy pork, fish, papayas, mangos, eggs, and other produce at cheaper prices than the supermarkets. The market was packed with people. I stopped at a small stall and bought two apples. I made my first monetary mistake by handing the seller three hundred and twenty five pesetas when it only cost me fifty. He lightly berated me in Spanish and I humbly took his lecture on proper money changing. I guess I wasn't that hungry as I left the Mercado and went back to the hostal.

I packed up again and started to dread the carrying of the bags. The pain was still there in my muscles and I was praying that I didn't cramp up. Now that would have been serious trouble. I left the hostal and only had to stop twice to reach the new hostal I was staying at. I got my room and put my bags on one of the two beds in my room. It was sparse but clean, and I was happy to have a window that opened out to a side street. Unfortunately I didn't have much time to rest, as my room hadn't been cleaned yet so I had to leave for a while until it was done. I decided to go look for my map and so I walked down Plaza de Mercado. It was a long, slanting street that was lined with various shops and cafes. Many people were walking here and there, most of them tourists. Then the street slanted the opposite direction and the name changed as well to Ave. Maria Cristina. This street was busier and there were even more people around. The cafes were more abundant and I could feel the tourist buzz around me. The sun was slightly covered by some thin clouds but it was still warm. A red digital sign read 23 C. I finally found a street vendor that sold maps and I got one for around 750 pesetas. Ah, and the price was on it too. If I had gone further, I could have gone to Plaza del Ayuntamiento. There was a magnificent fountain that I could see in the distance, and the waters rose and fell every so often. That was the heart of las touristas. Then I headed back to the hostal and my room was cleaned and ready for me. Still a bit tired, I decided I would rest for a few hours before venturing out in the early evening.

Side note- Toilets

So far, I have been in two countries and I have made an observation on the toilet facilities. In the hostel I was staying at in London, as you relieved yourself in the toilet (for men at least) you could get a grand view of suburbia London. The window was right above the toilet, so as you were waking up and emptying your bladder, London welcomed you with open arms. Also, for women who were relieving their bladders, as well as both sexes going number 2, I had to wonder if there was an angle from somewhere else where one could actually glance and spy in on us poor idiots while we were wiping. Hmmmm. As for Spain, I noticed the infamous bidet. I don't plan to use it, though I believe that it is more for feminine hygiene than male backside cleaning. Oh, and so far all the toilet facilities' light switches are outside of the room. Another snafu could be when one is on the toilet, and voila! The light goes out, it is late at night and alas, you don't know where you are. What a nasty trick the Spaniards have played on us tourists. More oddities from the road as the adventure continues.

Day 9

The bell rings out every hour on the hour, then rings singly on the half hour. The chatter of Spaniards reverberates across the small alley and into the open window. It is muggy and warm; one cannot sleep under the covers. The air is thick and it coats your skin like a warm wet towel. The light gets brighter and brighter as the day begins again in la ciudad Valencia.

I awoke a bit tired, as I was still getting used to the heat. Man, it is really humid here and I am still shocked by it. But, for some odd reason, I am not culture shocked by the new surroundings. I must thank Senoras Medlock y Murillo, my high school Spanish teachers. They were probably the best in the district, and I learned a lot those four years in their classes. Also, I am from California and that may help as well, since California has a major Hispanic (I use this loosely, as there are many different nationalities that speak and have a 'Spanish' culture like Mexicans, Guatemalans, Nicaraguans, and the other various Central American and South American nationalities) population, and also, the Spanish long ago colonized California itself. I still was having small problems with the language, but I was sure in time that I would speak a lot better and understand a lot more.

I changed rooms to another that had a bathroom and air conditioning, and for the price, it was a steal. Hell, I could have paid four times as much for the same room in the United States. So it was three weeks in this lovely room and I couldn't feel more content. After moving, it was time to explore the city. I had a marvelous time wandering through the streets, just walking around and seeing the 'real' Valencia. The cobblestone streets were lined with high buildings that had that distinct Spanish architecture. Small shops and cafes were the norm for these small alleys, hole-in-the-walls and calles. It felt really comfortable and enjoyable to just meander like a river to and fro'. I headed east and found myself at La Plaza de la Virgen, which was the main area for the most popular cathedrals in Valencia.

There was a service going on in Nuestra Senora de los Descamparados. It was a smallish church but full of character. There was a beautiful statue of the Virgin Mary made of gold and it glowed as if it were alive with the spirit of the Lord. I felt tingles throughout my body and I knew His presence was there. I felt out of place a bit because there was a sign that said you must not wear short sleeves or shorts, and of course that was what I was dressed in. I made a discreet exit and walked to my next destination, Cathedral.

The Cathedral was the holiest sight in Valencia, if not in this part of Spain. The myth was that this was the resting place of THE Holy Grail, the cup that Christ was said to have drank from and his blood collected into when he was crucified. I was tingling with excitement to see this. The Cathedral was surrounded by a magnificent square full of people and cafes. The Cathedral itself was a tear-inducing piece of unspeakable beauty. The mauve tower reached high into the skies and the whole place just vibrated spiritual power. I passed by a couple of beggars and I ignored them. It would grate on my mind afterwards. I entered the church, and the first thing I saw was the huge frescoes of many different people. Unfortunately, I didn't know most of these people, but the paintings were amazing just the same. There were displays of gold crosses, gold boxes and other various church artifacts and relics. There even was a preserved hand of a saint that was a martyr to for the Catholic Church dating back to the 1200's. Wow. I sat down on one of the wooden pews, which had a long plank connected on the bottom for prayer, and I said a prayer myself. I felt at peace and knew that no harm would come to me as the Lord was protecting me every step of the way. Put some coins in the alms box and as I walked out the doors I did give a little to the beggar that was leaning against the doors. He thanked me, and I thanked him for helping me be a better person. But for some reason I did not find the Holy Grail. I will have to come back again to see it.

I was off to find a cyber café. I wanted to check my emails and also see some of the news back home. Little did I know that I was in for the shock of my life. I found a hole-in-the-wall called Cyberdrac and I bought an hour's worth of time on the Internet. I checked my mails from home. I got one from my mom, one from my friend Jim and one from my other friend Candi. It was this mail from Candi that concerned me the most. She told me she had heard what happened in New York and Washington, and that they also shut down some major places in London. She wasn't very specific as to what had happened (she probably thought I knew what was going on all ready), but she said to take care and be very careful. And she said she was going to pray for the people that died. Died? I got up from my computer terminal and asked the attendant what had happened in The United States. She told me there had been some horrible terrorist attacks in New York and Washington. I rushed back to my terminal and went to the CNN news web site. In dark, bold letters the headline read, 'Attack on America'. I was stunned. There were smaller headlines reading how many feared dead, who could be responsible, a speech by the President citing 'a quiet, burning anger', and a headline that said 'The World is Stunned'. I was starting to understand the importance and gravity of the situation, and I started to read some of the articles. Apparently, there were four airplanes that were hijacked and sent to various places in the United States on 'kamikaze' dives. Two of them were into the buildings of the World Trade Center. One building collapsed completely, the other severely damaged. Another plane was sent to The Pentagon and it dove right into the building. Another hijacked airplane crashed before it could reach its determined target. A wave of fear, sadness and shock washed over me. I couldn't believe it. On American soil of all places. Thousands feared dead, including all of the passengers of the hijacked airplanes. My mind was struck with such numbness that I couldn't think straight. My heart fell into my stomach and I could feel tears well into my eyes. Even as I write this, it is hard to type the words, the devastating news still paining my heart. I looked up as many articles as I could, and viewed as many pictures as I could see. It was horrible. I couldn't understand why anyone would want to cause so much harm and pain. The world seems to always change like the weather. Sometimes it is warm and sunny; sometimes it is dark and rainy. It's raining right now. And also in my heart.

I left the café trying to cope with the tragic news of my own country. Here I was, in beautiful Valencia, and many of my countrymen and women were dead or injured. The nation was in a state of shock, as it was when the bomb exploded one morning in Oklahoma City. My God, what have us humans done to each other? I needed to escape. I found a super Mercado and bought some water and a liter of beer. Then I bought a cold beer at an outdoor bar and tried to be happy. I knew though, that I had to deal with the sadness. So I drank my beer quickly, tried to find an American newspaper (which I didn't find) and went back to my hostal. I saw the local paper in Valencia with a front page exclusive of the attack on The United States. There was a full-page picture of the damaged World Trade Center buildings and the headline read in Spanish, 'Ataque a Estados Unidos', or Attack on The United States. The smaller headline below it read that it was the single worst terrorist attack in the history of The USA. I browsed through the paper and it had quite a few pages of the incident. I couldn't read anymore so I took a hot shower and opened my beer. It was time to escape.

Day 9 Supplement

Do you ever wonder why the human race created beer? Or even wine and other alcoholic beverages? I don't know too much about the history of the creation of these potable liquids, but here's my theory about the reason why.

God, in his infinite wisdom, knew the future of humanity. He knew we were capable of such beautiful creations, and such destructive force. So, he gave humanity the invention of creating alcohol. He knew that we, as imperfect beings, could not cope fully with the tragedies or the destruction we could wreak upon the world and ourselves. And alcohol was something that could ease the reality of our destructive nature. Look at the monks. They drank wine. Why? They had to listen, day after day, to the sins of the world. Who

189

wouldn't want a drink after hearing them? Or the police, when they see a murder scene or investigate some horrendous crime? I respect the police for their courage and strength. If I were a policeman and had to deal with all the shit they had to deal with, I would definitely hit the bottle. For those that do, I can relate. For those that don't, I commend you for your strength.

For the everyday, normal John or Jane, alcohol can be an escape for sadness, despair, and the reality of the real world. For myself, it has been useful to escape loneliness and sadness. Today, I was really sad. Fellow Americans, no, fellow human beings died yesterday. Innocent and unassuming, they lost their lives. Sometimes, when incidents happen like this loss of life, I always ask why? Why do people have to die like this? What has the world come to? How will this world ever change to become the ideal world that we all can live in peacefully, harmoniously? It tears my heart apart. I don't cry often, but today, I couldn't stop the tears.

I thought about her a lot today. I was watching a movie on my computer, lying on the bed. And I realized that the bed could hold two people. Her and I. Holding her in my arms as the cool air circulated in the darkened room. Her warmth flowing from her body to mine, and mine to hers. My nose in her hair, smelling the freshness of the shower still in it. Sigh.

Thank you God for alcohol. Without it I couldn't be human.

Day 10

Buenos Dias! It is another splendid day in the city of Valencia. The air is already warm and humid as I leave the hostal for another day of adventure. I have looked on the maps and have decided to check out a couple of places before I head to the beach.

El Jardin Botanico is the first botanical garden created in Spain. It was first open in 1802 and has been continuously visited by numerous people since then. I walked the short distance to the place, and at first I wasn't sure if it was a garden or not. I saw the sign signifying the garden, but it was on a building that looked more for business than a garden. I walked in and asked the guard where I could find the garden. He pointed in the direction of the inner building, and I thanked him. There was a broad opening at the other side of the building, and it was the garden. Wow, what a change from a building to a garden. After paying my 50-peseta fee, I walked on the sandy, rocky path that started immediately from the polished floor of the building. There was a long path that seemed to walk right into a jungle. Luscious green trees hung above scattered benches and hardly let any light in. I followed the path a bit, taking in the scenery and looking around. There were few people here. An elderly man was reading the newspaper; a mother was pushing her baby in a carriage. I saw a couple of middle-aged women talking frantically in Spanish and there was also a groundskeeper that was raking up leaves. Most of the garden was quite lush and full of various species of flora, mostly trees and plants. I didn't see many if any flowers at all. The further I walked into the garden the more it felt like I was stepping into another world. I could hear birds cooing in the distance and there weren't any people around the deeper parts of the garden. Then I happened upon a few greenhouses. I didn't look inside, but they were mostly smaller sized greenhouses and a large one. I finally found a place that I wanted to sit down, in the medicinal plants section, and sat down on a gray stone bench.

The shock of yesterday's news finally left my mind, and I was more interested in what was going to happen next. I am sure that if I were home I would have been glued to all forms of information; television, Internet, radio, trying to learn and understand all of the things that occurred and that were going to occur. I took some notes about my experience in the garden, and then I read the newspaper. Of course the main headlines would be the terrorist attacks in New York and Washington, and there would be countless articles of who did it, why, what happens next, and how the world will change because of this incident. I will not go into political ground for this, as I have my own beliefs and theories. But, my own simple observation is that this terrorist attack will not only make the United States stronger unilaterally, but also the world. It was, unfortunately, a wake-up call for everyone that peace is not easily kept or won. Even, as they say, the most powerful nation in the free world could not be protected by the cowardly, evil acts that occurred. I am sure there are other nations that are privately thinking; *now you know how it feels*. But I have complete faith that my country will pull itself together and make itself even stronger. And, I hope, that it will make the world stronger as well. We only have each other, and we must not take that for granted. What else do we have?

I left the peaceful garden content and happy, and I looked at the map at the next destination: IVAM. Actually, I forgot to mention the Torres de Quart. It is a piece of the remaining battlement of the city of Valencia. It is a towering piece of the stone gates, and it has been in place since the 15th century. The guidebook mentions that one can see the cannonball pockmarks in the stone, and it is correct. Those holes were huge. Thanks to the Napoleonic invasion during the 19th century for those historic holes.

IVAM, or Instituto Valenciano de Arte Moderno, is a gallery displaying some of the most amazing paintings of the 20th century. As I entered the large, modern building, I was awestruck by the sheer immensity of its displays. Eight galleries and countless paintings by noted painters Willem de Kooning, Valerio Adami, Miguel Navarro, and Eduardo Chillida covered the three-storied building. There were some other artists as well that had quite amazing paintings. The imagination stunned the mind. I was very impressed with de Kooning's work. The colors were vivid and bright, and I was trying with futility to comprehend and imagine what he saw when he created his works of art. Mind-stunning.

I was supposed to go to a couple of other galleries that were close by and a church, but I wanted to get to the beach. I tried to find an American newspaper (nope), and found the FGV or tram station. I was completely confused with the cost of a ticket and where I was supposed to go. Unfortunately, not many people spoke English so I had to try my luck on my own. After ten minutes of not learning anything, I broke down and acted the 'tourist' and asked a couple. They told me to put 135 pesetas into the ticket machine and press the letter 'A'. After that, put it into another machine, which stamped the ticket as valid, and then take the train that read 'Dr. Lluch'. I was guessing that was either the name of the tram that was going, or it was a stop on the route that would signify the direction. It was a stop on the route I found out later as I looked on the map on the top of the train. The tram took me through the northern part of Valencia. I saw many older buildings and plenty of cafes and restaurants. The tram even passed through La Universidad Politecnica. After fifteen minutes, the tram stopped at Eugenia Vines, and I got off. I could see the beach from the street. It looked quite clean and there weren't too many people there. I walked onto the beach, and there were wooden paths that were on the sand that led close to the water. The beach itself was dotted with blue and white umbrellas and there were what looked like stacked up lounge chairs next to blue and white tents. What the tents were for, I couldn't decipher. I found a nice patch of dark brown sand to stake out on, and I put out my towel and placed my belongings on top of it. A few minutes of putting on the suntan lotion, and I was ready to enjoy myself. I walked to the water, and this would be my first time going into the Mediterranean Sea. The water was a murky green, and I was sure that the water would be cold. Lo and behold! The water was lukewarm, even a little warmer than Hawaii. It felt good. I went back to my towel and proceeded to bake my skin.

I have always heard the rumor that women in Europe would take off the top part of their bathing suits and act as if everything was normal. I had seen pictures of women tanning their bare breasts, but I thought nothing of it. Until now. I was actually surrounded by bare breasts and thong bikinis. I hadn't seen so much flesh exposed. There were two women on my left both naked from the chest up, wearing thong bikinis, and a woman behind me was topless as well. Hell, even the family in front of me let their bra straps down, though they didn't take off their tops. The funny thing was, it registered in my mind, but it didn't really faze me. Europeans…

I stayed for a couple of hours swimming in the warm Mediterranean and sunbathing with topless women on the beach known as Playa de la Malvarossa. I don't think I could have been more content. As with all good things, it had to end and I headed back to downtown Valencia for some cold cervezas and some much needed rest. And a cold shower.

Side note: I am writing this as an independent observation, and it is not intended to be a judgment on all Valencians. Maybe I should be flattered, but let me explain before I let you make your own judgment. I have been here for three days, and I have spoken English for 3 minutes. If that. 99% of the time I have been speaking, reading or listening to Spanish. Not that it bothers me. It is a strange phenomenon though, as all the big tourist gurus always say it won't be a problem if you don't know the language. I have no qualms whatsoever about speaking, reading or listening to Spanish. In fact, my philosophy is, *when in Rome do as the Romans do*. And I have thought to myself, that this is THEIR country, so therefore I must speak, read, and listen to THEIR language. It wouldn't be different if a foreigner came to the United States. They would most likely have to know English, and at least speak it to get anyone to help them. But the gurus say everyone speaks a little English in Europe. I am guessing, and this is not to inflate my ego, that they have accepted me more in their language than anything else. That, or they don't want to speak English. Hmmm. But I don't believe that. At least, not yet.

Day 11

It was going to be another slow day for me. I was going to check my emails and also go shopping for some real food. Since I have been in Valencia, I haven't eaten anything solid except apples and a Powerbar. Oh, and some pistachios too. I don't know why I hadn't either sat down for a traditional Spanish lunch or even bought more food at the supermarket; I guess I wasn't hungry or thinking. Either way, my hunger was starting to get stronger. My aunt gave me this mini rice cooker and I decided to use it. I wrote out a list of what I wanted and needed, and then packed for the beach. Yes, it was another day at the beach. I just wanted to relax and get out of the city. Not that I was tired of the city, but wherever I am, if there is a beach I have to go as much as possible to it. I walked out into the sunny, humid Valencia morning and walked down to the Internet café. My bearings for the city had become clearer, and I had a confident feeling of finding my way around it. It took me ten minutes to get there, and even in those ten minutes I was soaked. Yes, it's THAT humid here. I sat down and checked my mails. I got one from my mom, who asked me to stay safe. I could understand her concern. Then I read a mail from my friend Jim. He was mad because the mail I sent him a couple of days ago was completely in Spanish. It must have been because I was writing the mail on a Spanish computer and it translated all of my words to Spanish. I laughed out loud and thank goodness there wasn't anyone around to stare at me. He also wrote me that he was eager to come visit and I was excited about that.

Terri was a girl from Austria. She sat down next to my terminal about five minutes after I arrived and we talked to each other in English. Yes! I hadn't spoken a word of English unless it was to myself or to my mom on the first night I was here. I enjoyed talking to her and she was friendly enough. She had just arrived on Wednesday and she was going to be living in Valencia for six months working as an au pair. I told her my story and we had a good conversation. She left after a half-hour and asked me if I would be here again. I said yes, on Monday, and I hoped to see her then. She said the same and left. Then a couple of American girls from near where I lived sat nearby. They worked in Britain on a student work visa for the summer and then were getting ready to go home, but not before exploring some of the continent. I finished my time on the computer and then headed to El Corte Ingles, where the supermarket was.

I bought two bottles of wine, a loaf of bread, two cans of corned beef and a bar of soap. The only thing I couldn't get at the supermarket was a corkscrew to open the wine. I whisked in and out and then I headed straight for the tram that would take me to the beach.

The beach today was the same as yesterday. It had people, sand and sun. I chose another place to sit and it was in between two crowds. I enjoyed my time sunning and swimming, though it wasn't as warm. There were wisps of white clouds painted across the light blue skies, and the sun would be covered every so often by these clouds. The whole time I was there, I didn't see any topless women, but when I was leaving there was a woman who had just taken off her top, and I saw another woman down the beach sunning herself, leaning back against a chair, and her tanned breasts glowing dark brown. I am sure you are wondering why am always mentioning the 'topless' thing, and perhaps you think I am obsessed with the topic, but as an uncouth American, I am still coming to terms with the freedom of optional clothing. A culture shock if you will.

I went back to my hostal as fast as possible because I was anticipating the feast I was about to cook. Well, maybe not a feast, but a nice cooked meal for once. I washed the rice and put it in the cooker to cook. Then I opened the wine and let it breathe. It was a 2000 vintage bottle of wine

198

called 'Don Mendo'. I couldn't decipher the bottle to tell
what kind of wine it was, but it was red. Finally, I opened a
can of corned beef and I skimmed off the top with a fork
and ate it. Mmmm, it tasted salty and beefy. The first beef I
had eaten in two weeks. After twenty minutes, the rice
cooker went off, and I took off the top. A cloud of steamy
water wafted into the air, and I heard the rice crackle. I took
out some rice and mixed some of the corned beef with it.
Was that good! I poured myself a small glass of wine and
tasted it. A powerful tangy taste coated my tongue and it
was quite delicious. So, there I was, sitting in my room,
eating a cooked meal, and drinking some good Spanish
wine. Doesn't have to be difficult to make something
simple.

Day 12

Today was a rest day. Para descamparse. I slept in, stayed
in my room all day, and just relaxed. I didn't even feel the
heat of the day at all as the air conditioning was turned on. I
half-opened the windows and let the sun shine in. I heard
the normal chatter and noise of the city and it was a little
louder as it was Saturday. I watched a couple of movies on
my computer and also read some of the leftover articles on
the week's newspapers. I ate another meal of rice and
corned beef, and I was content. The day went fairly quick
and I was anticipating the evening, because that was when I
would be making a call home. Seven o'clock came around
and I made the call home. Unfortunately, the telephone at
my parent's house wasn't charged, so every time I got a
hold of my mom on the phone it would cut out after thirty

seconds. A little frustrated by that and the heat of the telephone booth, I shook my head. Then my mom told me to call on my sister's telephone, and I knew that I would be able to have a conversation without interruptions. This was actually my first call home since the terrorist attacks, and I was eager to hear what was going on. My mom said it was quiet but a lot of people were still in shock. I told her I was all right and that there hadn't been anything really dangerous to Americans here, but she warned me to keep a low profile, which I had been doing so far. I talked to my nephew. He seemed a little confused as to where I was, but it was good to hear his tiny voice on the telephone. Then I talked to my sister Andrea. Actually, she should have been the one in Spain as she was the Spanish major graduate. I told her how I was doing in the Spanish lifestyle and how she would have been proud of me speaking Spanish all the time. All in all, it was good to hear from home. It is the most curious thing that you never know how much you miss someone or something until you aren't around them or it. And right now it was good to hear from home. Tomorrow is Sunday and I will be going to church. Which church, I don't know, but I will surely find one, as there are numerous ones in the area I am staying in.

Day 13

I woke up too late to go to church today. I felt bad about it, but I knew that I could go to church anytime, anywhere. It wasn't an excuse, but I knew my faith was strong. The day has been quite nice, but I am choosing to write all day. I am working on a few projects to keep my poetic and writing mind working. So, poetry and maybe a short story will be produced today.

I have been here for a week and I have to say that it has been an excellent experience being in Spanish culture. For myself, it hasn't been much of a change when it comes to surviving in a foreign city in a foreign country. I think there have been only a couple of things I wasn't used to. One was that Valencia, and perhaps all of Spain, doesn't have drugstores like they do at home. At home in America, these drugstores are you have-all-things type of stores where one can find everything that is needed in everyday life. But here in Valencia, there isn't such a type of store. It is broken down to the types of items that stores will carry what you are looking for, like if I wanted a corkscrew (which I mentioned earlier), I had to find an appliance store that specifically carried those types of items. The same with the pharmacies. The pharmacies here are just what they are; they carry medicines, items for the care of the body, and that's it. American newspapers have been very hard to come by. There are countless newspaper stalls, but I have not seen one newspaper from home. The closest I have gotten to an English written newspaper were the London newspapers The Guardian and The Independent. But other than that, everything else has been quite normal. I have enjoyed shopping for food in Mercado Central, the open air stalls market, and also at the supermercado at El Corte Ingles. I love walking in the quiet, narrow cobblestone streets, taking in the everyday life of Valencians. The beach has been lovely. There are actually only a couple of things I would like to do still. I would like to eat a plate of paella, the regional dish of Valencia, and I would also like to sit at a café, sipping a cappuccino, writing my poetry or my journal. I have two more weeks so I will have more than enough time to do whatever I want to do. I have looked at the map I have been using for my directions, and I have been around most of central Valencia. In fact, it would be hard for me to really get lost now, since I have walked almost the whole area. But I still may get lost…

Day 13 supplement

When I started my journey, I weighed approximately 165 pounds. My normal weight was 135-140 pounds. I started taking an anti-depressant called Paxil and one of its side effects was weight gain. I started taking Paxil from November of 2000 to around August of this year (2001). So I gained in the span of nine months around twenty-five pounds. And let me tell you, with my small frame and that extra weight, you could really see it. I mention this because after almost two weeks traveling in Europe, I have lost almost all of it. When I just looked in the mirror a few moments ago and saw that my face didn't look bloated and my stomach wasn't a giant cauldron pot, I really reflected about myself. Not only how I had changed physically, but also mentally and emotionally. Given that I have only been gone from home for two weeks and the major changes within myself and on the outside, I was pleased. But at the same time, I couldn't help but feel a little sad. It had been quite a long road for myself from these last nine months to now. Hell, back in November I was in the psychiatric ward at a hospital because, in my own words, I had 'given up'.

The following months were laced with fear, anxiety, hopelessness and uncertainty. Along with my own mental problems, the voices (perhaps another mental problem) were strong in their negativity and I was certain that my life was not going to be as happy as it was in the past. The past felt more like a different life, and I had forgotten how it was to be able to think clearly and smile when I felt happy, or to be able to function as a normal human being. It is when I am writing that I feel most at peace, as I can express myself to the fullest and it is the only way I can express my passion for life. If you were to observe me in real life, you would think I was a quiet, unassuming person who may come off as a bit chilly. But I am the type of person that likes to keep to myself unless there is a time where I can talk or present myself. I have changed in that regard.

I used to be a cheerful, happy-go-lucky person who would go out of his way to meet people. I can still make friends easily but I choose, more or less, as to whom I approach nowadays. Not out of paranoia or mistrust, but my observational skills have been heightened to know whether or not to approach someone I would like to talk to. I have also changed in my demeanor. I used to be very expressive with myself. Saying hello to strangers and introducing myself to strangers was something normal for myself. Now, it is how I have described it earlier; I am more reserved and, I guess you could say, cautious. But I don't attribute it to only myself, but to the world as well. The world has changed a lot. It has become a world full of walls, and paranoid souls guarding these walls. It has become a world where it is better to have a suspicious eye than a friendly one. In some ways, I feel that my innocence was betrayed when I saw the world in this mind frame. But perhaps it was a blessing in disguise, so that I could at least protect myself from the evils of the world. But I haven't given up on good though. There still is good out there, you just have to find it. Unfortunately, in my mind, there is more evil than good. Let me give you an example. Here in Valencia, I have noticed that when the church doors are closed, they are thick, black iron doors that seem to be impenetrable. That tells me a lot. Or the iron bars on every window on the first floor of a children's hospital. Even my room has a set of boards that lock tight behind the windowpanes. London was worse. On top of some lower buildings, there was barbed wire, and in some cases, broken glass with the sharp tips pointing upward. There were numerous cameras perched on corners, stoplights and posted underneath overhangs of buildings. That should tell you a lot about the world we live in. And it is sad. But I won't give up hope that things can change for the better. That the world can become a place where we will all be able to live in harmony and peace. Most would shake their heads in disapproval, and rightly so with the present situation staring in our faces, no, slapping us in the face. But I believe, with all my heart and soul, that someday, the world will be the ideal world we all would want to have. And I will never give up that hope. I pray that I will do my part to move towards that goal and be recognized as a human being who did things to make the world a better place for all, and to change humanity so it there will be more good than evil.

Day 14

Officially two weeks on the road. So far, I feel pretty good
about it all. My weight has gone down, I have gotten into
better shape, and I have been able to function almost
normally in another culture. With the weekend behind me,
it was time to go out into the streets. I had an errand list,
and I departed early to finish it. The first thing was laundry.
I wasn't able to accomplish that, as the Laundromat was
closed and it wouldn't open for another fifteen minutes. I
couldn't even spare that much time. I rushed down to the
post office to mail off my postcards to the US, and then it
was off to El Corte Ingles to shop for more food. I took
about ten minutes in the supermarket and then I went out to
find the cyber café. Usually I will shop after I go to the
cyber café, but since my directions were the exact opposite
of my usual route, the cyber café would be the last stop. I
got lost for a half-hour, and then I had to wrap around the
center and cut through the middle so I could get onto the
street that I usually went down to the café. I found it easily
and walked up the steps. I looked left and there was Terri
on the computer. I was surprised that she would still be
there, as it was eleven already. I told the attendant I wanted
an hour and I sat next to Terri. We both said hello to each
other and asked about each other's weekend. She went to
the beach; I stayed in. She seemed in a good mood and we
chattered off and on for about forty-five minutes. Her time
was up before mine and as she got up to leave I asked her if
she wanted to do something sometime. She countered with,
"What are you doing after this?" I said nothing, and we
agreed to do something together after I was done on the

computer. She would return to pick me up in fifteen minutes.

I waited outside in the warm Valencian sun for her. She arrived a couple of minutes later and we decided to go to El Mercado Central. She had been there before but she wanted to have a better look. I was happy to finally have a companion on the journey.

As we walked the streets, we found out more about each other. She was eighteen, and she was from a village northwest of Vienna. She was au pairing for a Spanish family that ran a pharmacy, and they had three children for her to look after. She told me her parents were teachers, and she actually attended the school that her father taught in. She didn't like it very much as she told me that if she was out of line or not doing well, her teachers would talk to her father about her. We got to the Mercado and it wasn't busy. She bought two purple plums and two golden plums. As she ate one I told her about my reason for being in Valencia and about my journey throughout Europe. She was quite impressed with me being a writer, but I was actually embarrassed. It was amusing all the same.

We headed to El Jardin Botanico, but when we got there it was closed. So, I asked, would you like to go to Los Jardines del Turia? She agreed and we walked north to them. On the way we ran into some school children leaving class. It was probably kindergarten as it was almost twelve. As we got closer to the gardens, we saw the IVAM exhibit. We tried to go in but it was closed on Mondays. So we kept our heading to the gardens, which were only a couple hundred yards away.

The air was hot, but not as humid as usual. I was enjoying my time with Terri; it was good to spend time with her. We went down a ramp that led down into the park, and after a few minutes walking on the sandy path that ran parallel with some thick pine trees, we sat on a concrete bench and took a load off. The sun was covered by the trees, and except for the plentiful damn flies that seemed to stick on us like glue, it was a nice, peaceful place to relax.

We talked about everything. We talked about her boyfriends, my girlfriends, what we would want in the future, and also how our lives were turning out for the moment. Terri was quite intelligent and witty. It was an extreme pleasure conversing with her. So we sat there for a good hour or so, talking, discussing, and chattering. Then it started to get hot and I asked her if she would like to go somewhere else. She mentioned that she would like some ice cream, and that sounded really good. So we headed off looking for an ice cream shop.

There was one that was north of El Cathedral. It was a gelato shop that had numerous choices in flavors. I picked out a couple, Terri picked out a couple. I bought for both of us. She seemed to be surprised, but I told her it was all right. I looked at the time, and it was three. She was late getting back to help with lunch, but she said it would be fine. We walked down the street eating our melting gelato, and as she stopped to get ready to cross the bridge that would take her home, we agreed that we would do something tomorrow. I smiled and said goodbye, and headed back to my place, content and happy.

Day 14 Supplement

All we have is each other.

Human companionship. Is it that which we crave most in this world? *All we have is each other.* When you walk on the street, all alone, what is it that you wish most? To not walk alone? To be with someone to share your life, to share a simple walk on the streets? *All we have is each other.* When you feel the warm sun on your face and deep inside your heart, all you want to do is cry with laughter, cry with joy? And to be able to share that same feeling with someone else? *All we have is each other.* Human minds and human souls are so fragile, we take it for granted that our 'powerful' physical selves will always be the strongest. But only with each other can we be truly strong enough for the past, present and future. *All we only have is each other.* Thank you for humanity and its compassion, for without each other, we would all be dead inside.

I remember a day, in San Francisco, when I had lunch with my friend Jim Pacelli. We were sitting on a wooden table, eating a burger and fries right next to the ocean. It was a rare clear and mild day in midtown San Francisco. We were talking about our lives. I told him I was giving up alcohol for good. It was time to let my liver heal. I didn't want to die knowing that through my foolish choice of drinking I would destroy my physical self, and therefore end my own life. How could I look at myself ten, twenty, thirty years down the line, knowing I had already killed myself from drinking when those whom I loved would surely suffer because of my death? I remember when I told Jim that, there was a man, who was perhaps in his fifties. I wasn't sure if he had heard my words (and it wasn't my intention to let him hear my words), but he walked away. Earlier he was acting a bit daft, as if he were playing a part of the village idiot. Or the village drunk. Well, it was if my words rang true to him, and he didn't want to hear them. He walked off soberly. As for myself, it is sad to report that, in my present condition, I have not given up alcohol. Unfortunately my mind and soul are too fragile for the harsh reality of the world that we have made for ourselves. And the only escape I have is the sweet (or bitter) bliss of what is contained in the green bottle that contains a vague colored liquid. That's a funny thing, isn't it? A vague colored liquid. As if even the vagueness of the color of the liquid I imbibe is to trick the senses, to change the environment. Or to escape. But, I do hope that that man has finished his days drinking the vague colored liquid. Then he would be truly a strong individual. Stronger than me…

Love lost. Love found. Love lost again. Please excuse me if this sounds so melodramatic. It's the vague colored liquid that has stolen my mind and taken it to places other than the place I am right now. But the only consolation I can take from being drunk, is that it takes me back to the time when I was most happy. Sad as it may seem, it is true. I was lying beside her, in the middle of the night. The soft moonlight shone its beams through the skylight; there wasn't anywhere else I wanted to be. How could alcohol be more intoxicating than smelling her sweet, freshly washed auburn hair? Or to see her dark brown eyes looking into mine in the cover of the night? It doesn't seem so real. It seems as if it was only a dream I dreamt so long ago. Well, I think I'd better finish here. The rest is for me, and me only.

Day 15

I spent another day with Terri. First, though, I finally dropped off my dirty laundry and later I would pick it up and take it home. It was ten in the morning, and the weather was grim. The thick dark clouds in the skies were calling for rain, and I was pretty sure it would. Terri told me it was sunny 300 days out of the year in Valencia. Unfortunately for us, it was one of the 65 days without. We met at the cyber café, and then we headed to the Jardin Botanico. It would be open today, and so we walked to it in relatively quick time. We explored the garden, meandering through the almost empty paths and just taking in the tranquility and peace. We stumbled across a couple of places I hadn't seen on my first visit to the garden, and it was a welcome surprise. The first place that was new to me was an open green house that had trees and plants native to Africa and The Americas. It was almost like we were in the jungle, hiding from the animals, it was so real. And it was peaceful.

The second area that was new was a huge cactus garden. There was every cactus plant imaginable, from The Southwest USA, to Mexico and also other parts of the world. It was amazing that these plants were so self-sufficient and survivalists. Then we strolled around the rest of the park enjoying the time spent with each other. I was having a great time spending time with Terri and I was content. After the park, we headed to IVAM again so Terri could see the contemporary galleries of the artists there. We spent an hour looking at almost all of the works of the artists there. I, of course, had seen them all before, so I wandered around the rooms seeing what I had missed before. It was more fun the second time around.

After mind overload from the art museum, we wanted to get something to drink at a café. As we left the museum, tiny droplets of water started to fall from the sky. It wasn't really raining, but the water was coming down. We found a nice, quaint café near La Plaza de La Virgen and I had a cappuccino while Terri had this milky liquid that looked very much like a shake. Two strangely shaped cookies came with her shake, and we talked a bit about life and everything else that came to mind. After we finished our drinks, we decided to head to Filmoteca, or the movie theater. We were hoping to get out of this unfortunate weather and maybe see a good flick. We found it easily, but the theater did not open until six in the evening. So, since we were so close to the city center, we found a quiet bench and sat down and had a really good conversation about life, and also what we would like to do about changing the world. Terri also talked more about herself; how she felt inside and how she viewed the world in her own eyes. She was finally opening up to me and that made me feel more at ease; she was beginning to trust me. I had trusted her from the beginning, and for myself, it was easy to talk to her about almost everything.

Sadly, the time had come where she had to go back to her au pair job, and we planned to go to the beach together on Thursday. She was going to enroll in a Spanish class on Wednesday to sharpen up her Spanish, and it was going to take time to look into it. So, tomorrow I would be alone, and most likely would go to the beach, if it were sunny. My legs tired from walking, it was nice to be able to relax and put my feet up in my room. An hour later I picked up my laundry. Then I soaked my feet in warm water in, I guess it was, the bidet (!). It was actually sparkling clean, and I put the black rubber stopper in the drain. Then I filled it up with the warm water and placed my road-weary feet in it. Ahhhhhhh... It felt soothing. I listened to my music and sat back and finally emptied my mind of the day.

Side note- Food And Drink

I later looked in my guidebook, and I found out what Terri drank and ate at the café. She was drinking a beverage called 'horchata', which is a local drink made of pressed 'chufas' or tiger nuts. The cookies she ate are called 'fartons' (hehehehe), but they are buns, not cookies. Interesting...

Side note- Death

Are we so afraid of death? What is it that makes us afraid of our own mortality? Is it that we really don't know what will happen after our souls depart our bodies? I have never been quite afraid of death throughout my life. I don't know why, perhaps it is my strong faith in God and that He will take me to Heaven when I do depart this world. It is sad though, that there are way too many ways to die. Violent death has to be, of course, the worst way to die. Homicide is the worst thing one human can do to another. How can one rationalize taking another's life, especially using violence? I can't quite, and most likely won't, understand that mentality. Then there is death by natural means. I group medical deaths (cancer, brain tumors, and various other medical cases) with the natural death of oneself by either age or time. Time, meaning it was time to depart this world. Like a baby dying of SIDS, or dying in one's sleep. Only God knows why the method and the time of our deaths. Tomorrow, I could be run over by a car. Or shot, stabbed, beaten and/or any other means of dying. Perhaps I won't wake up tomorrow morning and see the sunshine piercing through the clear glass windows. Who knows? But I wish I could tell people that they shouldn't be afraid to die. We do what we can do with our lives while we can, when we can. Our lifetimes are not infinite, and sooner or later, death will come to us all. It is, as I have said earlier, how and when. Until then, we must live the best lives we can, each and everyday, and never be scared.

Day 15 Supplement

Most of our lives, we leave so much unfinished. Is that human nature? Or does it just mean that we have so much in our lives we can't possibly finish everything we start? There are times, though, instead of leaving it unfinished, it is time to walk away. I have always had a hard time walking away, mostly from the past. When you have memories so sweet and fresh that you still want it as such, it is hard not to let go of the past. Everything I ever knew and loved about Tiffany was in the past. That was eight years ago. Sure, we kept in contact; we wrote, we called, we sent pictures. But the time that has passed between her and I has been more than two thousand miles and different lives away. I have tried, in those eight years, to move on, to move forward. I've been with other women since, but the feeling was never quite the same. In fact, it was never even close. Only the vivid memories I had with Tiffany were the only link to those happy, happy feelings and the time I felt most free. Tonight I was thinking to myself. Why can't I let go of her? I know that she has changed. I know she isn't the woman I loved so dearly what seems ages long ago. I don't even know if we could even look each other straight in the eyes. My problem is, that we are still friends. That is something I cherish very much, it doesn't come without the pain of the past. Do I need to set myself free by letting her go completely? I am in dire conflict about this. I could free my soul, but I would lose a friendship. As I was thinking about this, I was also thinking about Tiffany and our whole time together. Though I refuse to say anything bad about her, I remembered the bad traits as well as the good. It had been a very, very long time that I had remembered those bad traits. And I really thought about them. I felt a little sad. I correlated my life with hers after she left London, and those bad traits were still there, even now. Am I trying to find an excuse to walk away? Or am I truly trying to rationalize the decision to say goodbye?

There were many times I would imagine talking to her on the telephone, and just finishing it all. To say what and how I felt, and then say goodbye. Oh, that would be the cowardly thing to do. And it wouldn't be fair. But I know it would close the door for all time on the pain and suffering I put to myself by holding on to her. The only thing that kept me holding on was the infinitesimal chance that we would meet and be together again. But, as I said before, things change. Lives change. It's funny, however, that she never married. I would have bet my fortune, if I had one, that she would have been married at least by now. But, she isn't. I don't know why.

I need to stop suffering. If I keep going on as I have, I'll most likely have a breakdown. I know I'd rather be on my own and stick to my chivalric mentality and hold on for Tiffany. But all it will do is destroy me in the end. I can still be on my own and not hold on to her. The question is, do I let go? And, will I be making the right decision? I know I can find someone else and have what I had with Tiffany. Not exactly the same, but I know there is someone else out there for me to love, and her to love me. I just have to find her, or maybe she'll find me. But until then, I must deal with the present situation, and I hope I find the right decision in my heart soon.

Day 16

Yesterday was the one-week anniversary of the worst terrorist attack on American soil. I was enjoying my time with someone while my American brethren were standing at a moment's silence for the victims of the attack. This morning I bought a couple of English newspapers and started to read intently the articles that had been spawned by that most horrible incident last week. There were talks of a coalition going into Afghanistan to either kill the main culprit of the terrorist attacks, or to punish Afghanistan itself. I wasn't too sure how I felt about this. Then there were other articles that pertained to the Muslim backlash from the attacks. Meaning, that non-Muslims were preying upon Muslims because the accused (and deceased) perpetrators of the attacks were Muslim. I shook my head and felt a pang of deep sadness in my heart. This is what I can never understand about the human mind. It just doesn't make sense, because we, as humans, are supposed to have the highest intelligence of any living thing on this planet. Even then, we cannot use our superior intelligence to think and make rational judgments. There was a picture that had a wall which was spray-painted in red; 'AVENGE U.S.A. KILL A MUSLIM NOW.' There were numerous articles reporting hate crimes against innocent Muslims in Great Britain and America. One in particular deeply hurt me. There was a 28 year-old Afghan student who had just started to drive a taxi to make money for his college tuition. He was on his second night on the job, and in the early morning hours, he picked up three men. These men proceeded to drag him out of the taxi and severely beat him. They beat him so badly he was paralyzed from the neck down. The paralyzed driver's brother was quoted as saying that he 'is a very calm and well-behaved boy. He is first class in the family, always polite and to everyone and thoughtful.'

Back in 1941, there was a terrorist attack on America. In the morning of December 7th, the Japanese Imperial Navy sent in airplanes to disable and destroy the naval fleet at Pearl Harbor, Hawaii. Many American lives were lost that day, and many tears were shed for them. But afterwards, certain citizens of the United States, Americans in their own right, were herded together and sent off to concentration camps across the Midwest and Western USA. There were many articles that suggested that they were spies. Picture diagrams would depict how to single out these 'supposed' spies. Most of these citizens were law-abiding, and some had farms and stores. Windows were broken, racist slogans were painted across doorways and walls. My grandfather was 21 years old when his train pulled out of the station and headed to Topaz, Utah. He blankly stared out of the cattle car that took him and countless others to the concentration camp that would be his home for almost five years. I also had many other relatives that were placed in these 'internment camps'; that was the word the government used. My family has and always will call them concentration camps. That was sixty years ago. Even though it is the 21st Century, old habits are hard to break.

I don't know what will happen. Who does? We live, day by day, trying to get through the day without harm, without conflict. I hope that everything will turn out all right when my country decides what to do. I am a pacifist by nature, so I don't condone violence of any kind, for any reason. But, I trust that my country will do the right thing. Peace and compassion is all I ask for, but it seems we, as humans, cannot even achieve that. But I will never give up hope that it will happen. Someday.

The sky has been gray and dreary all damn day, and I wanted to go to the beach. No chance today. It's a sit and read a book day. Or listen to music day. Or anything indoors day. Anything but going to the beach day.

Oh, I did get a chance to go back to El Cathedral and saw the Holy Grail. It is encased in a glass box, and the cup itself is a gold chalice. It is hard to get a real good look at it, as it is on a wooden mantle that is cordoned off. It is in a small side room that has pews, like a small church. I wasn't too impressed, but it was an enlightening sight nonetheless.

Day 16 Supplement

It has started to rain. I heard it first instead of seeing it. The drops came down heavily, thumping against the rooftops and down onto the gray cobblestones. When I was a child, I used to think that when it rained, it was God's way of washing away the evil stuff that had dirtied everything. And much good it did when the grass would leap from the ground, its deep emerald color a beautiful sight in the gray. Or when the sunshine would finally break through the siege

218

of rain; the rainbow that would arc the skies could bring a soothing feeling to the soul. But, as I got older, my thoughts would be that it would rain because it was God's way of warning humanity that we were getting too apathetic; the world was becoming more evil and less good. In the good book, it does tell the famous story of God flooding the earth because there was too much evil going on in the world. And, after He cleansed the earth with His waters, He promised never to do that again. And that is why there is a rainbow. It is a sign of his promise. And such a beautiful sign it is.

I opened a bottle of wine, more to relax than to escape, and I realized, that when America was attacked in New York the first time, it was in 1993. That was when I was in London. And now, eight years later, I am again abroad. I wonder if this is some sort of strange coincidence…

Day 16 Supplement II

Thunder and rain…that's what I'm hearing now. The light of the day has been gone for awhile now, but the rain hasn't left since midday. Now there is thunder, but I haven't seen lightning. It's coming down steadily, heavily.

We live in a dream world,

A world where there are no boundaries,

Freedom is for all,

Sleep is readily available,

The bliss of peace

Is taken for granted.

It's supposed to be the same tomorrow. Clouds and rain. Usually, weather like this would make me feel depressed or sad. But tonight, I feel hope and wanting. I feel that I want to stand out in the rain and feel the droplets drip onto my tired body, to cleanse the dirt that has collected on my soul. And feel the hope of a brand new world…

Side note- Speaking

I finally found out why Spanish people only speak Spanish to me, and rarely, if ever, speak English. When I bought a bottle of water at a small café nearby my hostal, I was trying to find out how much it cost, because the woman spoke so fast. After three times, she repeated the cost of the water in English. I was surprised, because I had spoken to her a few times in Spanish before. She told me that not many people spoke English. 'Poco', she said, or little. I finally understood. At the same time, I felt a little betrayed, because I had spoken Spanish most of the time, as if I were Spanish as well. But now I had broken the language barrier by adding English to the Spanish. And the mystique of 'When in Rome, do as the Romans do' was not as special. Alas, the crude American has woken up in me…

Day 17

I'm tired. No, I am REALLY tired. It's mid-afternoon on a nice, sunny Thursday. I just spent the day with Terri. We were supposed to go to the beach, but when we met at the

220

cyber café, the sun was absent and the dark clouds were present. I wasn't sure if it was going to rain, but it sure looked like there was a good chance of it. So we decided that we would stay in the city and figure out something. She opened her map and there were a few choices we had; there was a 'hippie' market somewhere near El Mercado Central, and we could see that. Then there was also Museo Nacional de Ceramica, or the National Museum of Ceramics. Finally, there was la Ciudad de las Artes y de las Ciencias (City of Arts and Sciences), which was a planetarium, IMAX cinema and laser show all in one. We opted for the hippie market.

 The streets were still wet with the last night's rain, and there were small puddles of water and mud here and there. It was hard to avoid all of them. As we walked through the narrow streets between the tall, crumbling buildings, we ran into numerous tourists and passersby. It was almost eleven in the morning and the city was alive and well. We meandered for almost a half hour until we realized that there wasn't a hippie market, but more likely the market was only open certain days. So, feeling a bit tired, we sat down at an outdoor café and I had a café con leche while Terri had chocolate milk. I showed her some of my writings on my laptop (I am typing this on it right now), and some of my poems. She enjoyed them and I was happy about that.

After the café, we decided to go and get more of my writings on a disc from my room and then go somewhere peaceful where she could read them. Hurriedly I went to my hostal room and got the disc, and then it was west to el Jardin Botanico again. We got there and the opening was cordoned off. There was a sign saying that because of the rain, everything in the park was too wet so it was closed. So, we headed north to the Jardines del Turia. As we headed to the park, the clouds started to part and the sun finally showed itself. Ah, it was warm and delicious. I had to take off my long sleeve shirt, and Terri also took off hers. We found a lone concrete park bench that had a couple of small puddles on it, and sat down. The longer we stayed in the park, the clearer the sky became. It was really nice. As was our usual pastime, Terri and I talked and talked and talked. We talked more about life in general. She was telling me that her schedule was difficult to get used to. It wasn't a fixed one. She had to get up early in the morning to get the kids ready for school, and help clean the house. Afterwards she was able to have 4-5 hours for herself, and then she had to help with the kids in the afternoon and sometimes late into the evening. It was wearing down on her and I could tell she was not very happy. Then all of a sudden she became quiet. I looked at her face, and I saw tears coming down. I was quite concerned. I took out a tissue and gave it to her. She thanked me and wiped her face. She was missing home, she was missing her boyfriend, and she was trying to deal with her new life. I could relate…

I tried cheering her up with some of my funny stories. I don't know if it worked or not, but it seemed that she was a little better. It was tough on me to see her sad. I felt the same way about home, Tiffany and the adjustment of my new life. I did my crying privately. But I cried too. I asked her about her home, and she told me about it. She told me it was on a hill, with a pond in the backyard. There was hardly any noise as her house was in a small village. Then she told me about her room. It was small, but there were many things in it. She could listen to music, draw, read and anything else that she wanted to do. I told her I would definitely come visit her. She was happy to hear that. I told her about my home in California, and my parent's backyard. It was a peaceful backyard, with a small lawn and trees surrounding it, with a fence covered in ivy. Sometimes, I told her, I would just sit and close my eyes, clearing my mind, or read. Then we talked about the desserts of Austria. I told her I saw many food programs that always had an Austrian dessert. She smiled and her brown eyes glinted in the sunlight. She told me that Austria had the best desserts in the world, and that sometimes Austrians would eat dessert as if it were a meal. She seemed a lot better now. Then it was time again for her to go back home.

We walked, quietly, back to the bridge that she crossed to go home. We talked about the death penalty, and our own thoughts on it. We both agreed that it was inhumane. Then I asked her if she saw half a glass of water, was it half-empty or half-full? She immediately said half-full. And then she asked me what would I say? If I were younger, I would have instantly said half-full. But, it's strange how our beliefs and views change, as we get older. I said it was both. She said of course it was, but what would I pick. I shrugged and said, half-empty. Then we silently walked the last few hundred yards until we saw her bridge crossing.

She was going to Barcelona from Friday to Sunday evening, so we made plans to go to the beach on Monday. We gave each other a hug, and as she walked over the bridge, I turned away and headed back into the city.

Now I'm sitting on the bed, finishing my day's writing. I am also waiting for the rice cooker to go off, so I can eat. I think that later I will write a letter to Tiffany. Yes, that would be nice…

Side Note- Terri

Terri's full name is Theresa. I really wasn't sure what her real name was, but she told me when I asked her about her email address. The first part of her address was Resi, and I was trying to find out what that meant. She told me Resi was short for Theresa, and Terri was another shortened way to say her name. I asked her which she liked best, and she said Resi, but Terri was just as good…

Day 18

It was a mostly clear morning on this Friday morning. The air was warm again, and the last couple of days of rain seemed to evaporate into the past. It was going to be a leisurely day for me. First, it was off to the post office to mail a letter to Tiffany, and then an hour at the cyber café to check my mails. Finally, the rest of the day would be spent at the beach. So I left early to go to the post office. It wasn't too busy on the streets and I slowly made my way down the streets at a leisurely pace. The sun was shining brightly, and it felt like it was going to be a great day.

I spent a half hour waiting in a queue at the post office. Either the workers were slow or there were too many customers. Either way it was not fun waiting my turn to just get a stamp to put on my letter. And when it was my time to move to the front of the line, it took me only one minute to pay the worker and get the letter stamped.

After the small inconvenience at the post office, next was the cyber café. I sat at my usual computer and I checked my mails. There wasn't any from home, which made me a little concerned. I did get one from my friend Jim and he was telling me that the news from the US was that the government was still beating the war drums and that an attack seemed imminent. I wasn't too happy about that. There wasn't anything else from anyone so I surfed the net for news on this proposed attack and other news from around the world. I didn't find anything interesting, so I looked up my usual sports web pages. After a half hour, there was a shadow behind me. I turned, and there was Terri. She had come in to check her mails before she was to go to Barcelona. It was a nice surprise. We sat together chatting and surfing the net. She got my email that was supposed to confirm that her email worked. And she also got my mail with the web page of my book on amazon.com. I actually spent an hour and a half with her. Afterwards, we both left together. I was headed for the beach and she was going to check on more Spanish language schools. So we said our goodbyes and we parted.

I walked north and crossed the Pont de Fusta Bridge that crossed into the northern half of the city. Then it was a quick ride on the tram to the beach.

The weather was really beautiful at the beach. The sunshine was out in force and there were scattered clouds across the light blue skies. I found a small patch of dark sand and had a nice time sunbathing. The one thing that mildly disgusted me was the numerous cigarette butts and dead flies strewn all over the place. With the rains the last couple of days, I guess the sand sweepers didn't have a chance to do their job since it was raining. I stayed a couple of hours, and I had a nice, peaceful time. And then it happened.

You know when sometimes, you could be having a great time enjoying your life, and then all of a sudden something occurs that makes it all go to shit? Well, it did for me. I walked back to the tram station and bought my ticket. I waited for the tram to pull up to the platform. I entered the last car and sat down. There were only two other people in the car with me. Then, as we made it around the loop that would take the tram back to my drop-off point, it stopped. Everyone, except me, got out. The conductor came and told me to get into the first car. There were three cars in all. I found a seat near the exit doors. And then a group of young youths came onto the train from the second car. They were staring at me as if they were going to come after me. One of them said 'Vale!' which means 'Get him!' I was a little concerned about that. I tried to keep to myself. Then a stop later, the tram police came on. They seemed to be there for a purpose, and I didn't put two and two together until I felt this wave of fear wash over me. It seemed that they knew something was going to happen, and they were there to make sure it didn't. Now I was really, really concerned. I sipped at my empty can of Coke, and kept my eyes glued to the window. There was a ticket checker, and he put a check on my ticket after I gave it to him. Then, for each stop closer to my own, I was starting to think. What if these youths are going to ambush me before I get to my hostal? My mind started to race and I was starting to plan in my head what I would do if I were going to be attacked. First, I would make sure the route I took back to the hostal was where there was a lot of people, even better would be tourists. Most of my route was through tourist sights. I usually would cut through the Plaza de la Virgen and then I would pass by El Cathedral. After that, it was through a couple of narrow, quiet alleyways and then right to Plaza del Mercado. A block later and my hostal would be on the left hand side.

I had a long cord for my earphones. Using this, I could at least defend myself a little. But what was the most important was making sure I wasn't alone on a quiet side street. The tram stopped at Pont de Fusta, my stop. One of the youths stood next to me in front of the exit doors for the last couple of stops. I was sure something was going to go down. So, I waited for him to leave. He got out and walked far to the right of me. I mingled with the rest of the people coming out of the car, and did my usual walk through the tram station/police station. My knees were a little weak and my heart was pumping furiously. I followed my normal route at the beginning, keeping my eyes open and watching anyone getting close to me. It seemed that everyone was staring at me, as if I were a 'hit'. I was not very happy. But I knew I had to survive and make it to my hostal. So, I made it through the first part of my route. Then, I changed course and headed towards the main thoroughfare Av. San Vicente Martir. It was a semi-crowded street that connected to Av. Maria Catalina, and then finally to Plaza del Mercado. I hurriedly walked through the streets and I was stuck behind a couple walking the same path as I. I could see my hostal as the corner turned left. Then I saw a group of people right next to the hostal I was staying at before. I thought at first it was them, but I was a little relieved as there were a few other people around. I could see the open door of my hostal, and I skipped up the porch and into the door, safe.

Was I hallucinating? Or was this something that was really going to happen? As I sit here and write this entry, I have to wonder. Piecing things together, it sounds very plausible. First, the conductor clears out the other two cars. If I were alone in that last car, what could have happened if those youths were to go into my car? And the tram police. Why, all of a sudden where they there? They really did look like they knew something. When I saw them come onto the train, it was like a signal, a sign to me. And then the youths themselves. They were there to accomplish something. And I don't think it was going to be something good.

You know, I wrote an email to my 'spiritual advisors' John and Linda Keough. They are both pastors for a new Christian concept called 'healing rooms'. What they do is invoke the spirit of God and pray for an individual in these rooms. They will pray to heal them physically, emotionally or mentally, or they will pray for the individual to 'save' them from their sins and the like. Not your conventional pastors, they are from the modern school of Christianity, and mix in some of the old teachings of the Bible to more of the current teachings. They 'saved' and 'blessed' me for the trip I am on now. Well, I am glad that I saw them. I think it helped in my survival today. Anyways, back to the email. I wrote them to thank them for their prayers and blessings, and that I would be eternally grateful to them. Then, I turned to a darker topic. I wrote to them that I was feeling an Evil presence near me. I told them that I couldn't explain it, but I knew it was close to me and following me. I knew for some time that there was some sort of Evil presence around me many times before, but today, in its most awful form, it reared its ugly head at me. I asked for guidance. And I waited for a reply. I haven't heard from them yet, but perhaps I should call them. Tomorrow is Saturday, and that is when I make my calls home. I am quite disturbed by this incident, and I will be thinking about my future plans from now until I talk to everyone at home…

I feel sad more than scared. It has come to my attention that my experiences with bad, or Evil, people have not been extensive. Actually, I have barely any experience with them at all except for that presence that has always been around me and a few isolated incidents. But I can truly say that I have been quite lucky in my life in regards to that. I think the hardest thing to realize is that there are always going to be these types of people, with the same types of mentality, and that in itself is a frightening thing. There isn't any way to rationalize with these types of people. They would slit someone's throat without thinking about it. Or gather around and beat the crap out an individual in a street alley. My fallacy, or gullibility is that I believe there aren't these types of people that will kill, maim, and destroy without a care to human life or humanity itself. Well, I am wrong in this case. There are people like that. And now, I am troubled with the circumstances that have happened to me, and perhaps will happen to me in the future.

Day 19

I fell asleep early with my Aunt's gift to me when I departed for Europe: The Bible Promise Book. This book contains passages of the Bible for certain things going on in one's life. I was steadily reading the passages for 'Fear', 'Courage', 'Comfort' and 'Death'. Yes, even for death. That's how scared I was last night. Today, I haven't eaten. I drank some water, chewed a little gum and washed my socks. Other than that I played some of the computer games on my laptop and bided my time until I could use the telephone. I had to wait until five o'clock in the afternoon my time, eight o'clock in the morning my family's time. I was still a bit scared to go outside. The voices were stronger now- and in Spanish. Matale. Vale. Abajo. Kill him. Get him. Down. I went down to the pay phone in the hostal. There was a girl in it already making a call, so I sat down and waited on the steps. She came out a couple of minutes later. She told me that it wasn't working and it took some of her money. I went in and shut the door. I took the receiver off the hook and heard the telephone vibrate and make a cranking sound. The small LCD screen was blank. And then after a few seconds the telephone was quiet. There wasn't even a dial tone. On the screen it read 'Por favor, espera.' Please wait. I put the receiver on the hook, and then took it off again. The same things happened again. I tried to press the clear button, but it didn't do anything. I got out of the booth and asked the hostal owner if the phone was broken. He said yes and that it wouldn't be fixed until Monday. Great. I had to go outside to the telephone tree at La Lonja, about three hundred yards away.

I went back to my room to put on my shoes, and then I sighed deeply. Lord please protect me. I walked with authority (though my stomach was weak and my knees felt like rubber), and exited the hostal. The air was thick and humid, and it was just starting to drizzle. I was on alert. I saw a guy standing near the Lottery booth. He seemed to be there doing nothing at all. I tried to make myself more comfortable and I said hello to him. He returned the greeting. I walked past him, and then remembered that there was a telephone in the hostal that I stayed at the first night I arrived in Valencia. So I ran up the steps and saw the owner at the front desk. I asked him if the telephone worked, and he nodded. I opened the door and a thick wad of heat splashed across my face. I closed the door and took the telephone receiver off the hook. A dial tone. Whew…

I dialed as fast as the automated program would let me. I went through the whole cycle in less than a minute, but I was still desperate to get the call through. I heard the call tone for my parent's telephone at home. *Please pick it up. Please pick it up.* After four rings the answer machine came on. After the beep I asked if anyone was home. Then I heard my mom's voice on the line. I almost broke down.

I told her I didn't feel safe in Valencia. I told her about the incident that happened the day before. I told her about the voices that were telling me these evil words. She told me that this seemed to happen all the time when I went somewhere. I told her it was true. She asked if I was taking my medicine. I said no. She said that might be the problem. I told her it wasn't in my head; it was all around me. She asked me what I wanted to do. I told her I wanted to go back to Hawaii. Maybe it wasn't my time to be here. Maybe I needed to get help again. She agreed. I told her I was scared to go outside. She told me that I would have to if I wanted to get back to Hawaii. I sighed and agreed with her.

If anything should happen to me, then I want you to.... No, don't say that. *Why?* Because Steve, you make it all sound so dramatic. *But mom, that's how fearful of my life I am.* Well, Steve, what do you want to do? *I want to leave.* Well, then you will have to make the plans and get everything done. *Ok.*

I talked to my sister Erin for a bit, and I told her what was happening. She told me I couldn't keep running away from the demons. I have to face them and defeat them, or else they will always follow me. I agreed. She told me I needed to get help- spiritual and mental. I didn't need to say anything to agree with her. She told me she would pray for me at church tomorrow, and that I should take care of myself.

My mom came back on the telephone and she asked me what I needed to do to get out of Valencia. I told her that I had to get a ticket back to Honolulu. I still had the other part of my round trip ticket from London to Valencia, so I told her I could try getting it changed to the earliest date possible. Then I could get a one way ticket to Honolulu at London. She said it sounded ok. She said she would talk to my aunt and grandma about staying at their house for a couple weeks so I could get established. She would call me tomorrow. I thanked her and told her I loved everyone. She told me she loved me and to take care. And pray.

I walked back to the hostal feeling a little better. It was raining, and I made my way back quickly. There was a group of guys standing outside the hostal with the owner. He was giving them directions to somewhere. Then a group of girls came out of the entrance. I walked in and waited at the desk for the owner to come back in. He did and gave me my key. I hopped up the steps and into my room. I locked the door and started to look for my unused portion of the roundtrip ticket from London to Valencia…

Day 20

I awoke feeling tired and apprehensive. It was Sunday, and I had to wait until Monday to get my ticket changed. I didn't do much except for play some of the computer games and pack. I definitely wanted to make sure that I didn't waste any more time here in Valencia if I could get out of here tomorrow. The air-conditioning blasted its frigid cold air throughout the room and the lights were on. The shutters and windows were closed. I listened to music on my computer with the headphones, keeping my mind at ease from the voices. The day was uneventful. But it went slow. And I hated waiting, hiding. It finally became evening, and with my bags packed and all of my documents put in a pile on the table, I turned the lights out and slept restlessly through the night.

Day 21

I awoke early. I wanted to get down to the Iberia office by ten. Most every place in Valencia opened around ten, so I wanted to get there by the time it opened. I also had to go to the cyber café to log onto my bank account and transfer my money from the savings to the checking so I could buy my ticket to Honolulu without any problems. I changed and tried to put on a brave face. I decided that if I ran to the places I needed to go to, I should be all right. I didn't care if I looked foolish, because I was more concerned with my safety than my appearance. For the first time, I put on my running shoes. I had my ticket in my Bible Promise Book, and my blessed piece of cloth was in there as well. I decided also, that I wasn't going to wear my portable stereo. I had to make sure all of my senses were clear. Leaving the hostal, I felt the slow grip of fear grab my shoulder. The sun was shining, and the air was slightly warm and humid. Just as the hand of fear started to creep over my shoulder and into my heart, I sped out down the street, and the hand lost its grip.

The run was quick and uneventful. I kept my mind sharp and clear. My eyes did not meet any others; my legs kept going. My chest felt a little heavy, but I did not stop for a rest. I made it to the Iberia office in five minutes. As soon as I entered the office, sweat started to bleed out of my pores. I sat down and waited, as both sales agents were busy with other customers. I wiped some of the perspiration from my brow and the cool air in the office helped dry the rest. A couple of minutes later I was sitting at the first desk. I told the sales agent I wanted to leave today. He looked on the computer and said there weren't any seats. My heart dropped. I asked him if he was sure. He scratched his balding head and adjusted his glasses. *Un momento.* After tapping on the keyboard for a few seconds, he said he did find a seat. I was relieved. I handed him my original ticket and he wrote out another on. I paid a fee for the change, and then quickly left the office.

The cyber café was only a half-block away from the Iberia office. It was also across the street. I waited for almost five minutes, as the traffic was both heavy and stop-and-go. I finally found an opening and dashed across. The huge wooden doors to the cyber café were closed. I started to feel that hand on my shoulder again. I sat down, resigned to waiting until the cyber café opened. Actually, the café was supposed to be open already. Just my luck. About three minutes later, a couple of suited men walked out. But the doors were shut again. I started to read my promise book to keep myself calm and sane. Then a blonde-haired woman walked up to the doors. Then she sat down next to me. She told me the café usually opened on time. Her cell phone rang and she started to talk in German. Then the blinds lifted from the windows and the doors swung into the café. I rushed in and told the attendant I wanted a half hour. The first thing I did was to transfer my money. Then I wrote my mom a quick email about my plans. I had twenty minutes left, so I rushed through news web sites. But I didn't really read anything. I was burning up time, and I knew I was getting more and more nervous by the minute. I left ten minutes early, and ran back to the hostal.

Nothing happened. I made it back without incident, and I told the receptionist I was leaving today. He didn't know how glad I really was when I said those words. I brought my bags down from my room, and I went out to hail a taxi. I found one quickly and he whisked me out of downtown Valencia in a matter of minutes. I was relieved, but disappointed and a bit angry. I guess it wasn't my time to be here in Europe. I could always come back. Or maybe not.

The flight back was nice. I sat next to a couple of men from Northern Ireland. They offered their condolences for the terrorist attacks. I thanked them. They were on holiday to see the Formula 1 race in Valencia. I told them I was going back home. They understood. The airplane touched down at Heathrow at three-thirty. I was finally out of hell and back in cold, rainy London.

I stayed at the same hotel that I worked at eight years ago. The West 2 Hotel. I guess it was somewhat fitting to end my travels at the place I had started it so long ago. Kind of closing the book after the final chapter. I called my mom and told her I had made it. She was glad I was safe and sound. I told her I was still a bit scared, but she told me she had the utmost confidence that I would make it to Hawaii. I felt a little better. I told her I had to replace my passport and also buy my ticket to Honolulu. I was a little perturbed about the passport replacement, as I might have to wait extra days to get it replaced. She told me that I just had to do it and it would be all right. I said you are probably right. After I finished talking to her, I went straight to the ATM to get some money, and bought the last meal I would eat in London: fish and chips.

Day 22

I was up and out of the hotel door early. I called the US embassy and found out it was open at eight thirty. So I headed straight for the tube and took it to Marble Arch, the stop that the embassy was closest to. I walked out of the station and I, of course, went the wrong direction. I stopped at a hotel and the concierge gave me a map and directions. I followed them, and I was right outside of the embassy in ten minutes. There were swarms of London policemen in yellow jackets around the embassy. Most were talking into two-way radios or talking to passersby. I stopped next to one and asked him which entrance was for passports. He pointed to my right. I saw the steps that went up to the rectangular building. There was a man also holding a two-way radio, but he was dressed in a black suit and tie. I thanked the policeman and skipped up the steps. The man stopped me and asked what I wanted. I told him I was here to get a replacement passport. He pointed to the glass doors. I walked through and there was a desk with a white shirted guard behind it. I had to give him my backpack and portable stereo. Then I went through a metal detector. He said to go up to the doors to the right. There was a pair of glass doors and also an enclosed booth where a US marine was sitting and observing the immediate area. He controlled the locks on the doors and he let me through. I went to the desk that was right after the doors. A man with a British accent gave me a couple of forms to fill out. He told me I also had to get a couple of passport photos from down the street. After about an hour of going through the whole process of getting my new passport, I was getting a little stressed out. It was typical bureaucracy and paper pushing. I finally got my passport and rushed out of the embassy, looking for the nearest telephone booth. I found one close by, and made a call to a bucket shop (discount travel agent) for a one-way flight from London to Honolulu. There was one leaving tomorrow from Gatwick at noon. I took it and told the ticket agent I would be coming down to pick it up now.

With the freshly printed ticket in my backpack, I hailed a cab to take me back to the hotel. I was going to save time and book a hotel close to the airport so I wouldn't have to get all stressed out. I booked a room in the Holiday Inn, and called a cab to pick me up in ten minutes. Thirty minutes later, the cab finally came, and I rushed out of London and got just a bit closer to home.

The drive to the hotel was supposed to be an hour. It ended up being two and a half. The driver was from The Sudan. He was a really nice guy, but he didn't know where he was going. It didn't bother me much, but the longer we stayed on the road, the more I was getting worried. We ended up at the Holiday Inn after getting lost a couple times and asking probably four people on the road, and I was relieved that I had arrived. The skies were dark and cloudy as I dragged my bags into the hotel. It took a couple minutes to get my room, and a bellboy helped with the bags. As soon as I got into the room and shut the door, I collapsed on the bed, exhausted from the whole day's ordeal. But I didn't rest long. I rang my mom at her work and told her I had bought the ticket home and all I had to do was get onto the plane at Gatwick. She was relieved that I was almost home. Me too. I gave her my flight information to give to my aunt, and then I told her I would call her when I got to Houston. Houston was the first leg of my two-leg flight. I was to leave Gatwick at noon and arrive at Houston, Texas at four-thirty that afternoon. Then I had to stay over in Houston for the night, and finally I would get on the plane to fly seven hours to Honolulu. After hanging up the telephone, I made some tea and watched television for the rest of the evening.

Day 23

I awoke at five in the morning. I think I was just really nervous about missing my flight, so I had my internal clock working a couple of hours ahead. I packed the rest of my luggage and waited until six. Breakfast was brought to my room at that time. It was a tray with a plate of eggs, bacon and sausage. There was fresh fruit, a croissant, a health bar, and cereal. I ate as much as I could and then watched a little television. When the time was seven, I took my bags down to the lobby and paid my bill. I waited outside for the express bus to Gatwick. The air was misty and cold, and the sun couldn't be seen in the sky. I waited with a couple from Israel, and they asked me where I was going. I told them my story, and they told me they were going to Croatia. The bus came roaring into the parking lot, and I boarded it, paying a couple of pounds for the fare. Then the bus went onto the street, headed for the airport.

I didn't think about too much at this point. All I wanted to do was get on the airplane and get back home. The rest of the time from now until I got on the airplane was mostly waiting, waiting, and more waiting. I did get checked over a couple of times for security reasons. That took me by surprise, but I understood why. It would most likely be the same when I got into the US, since the terrorist attacks had made security at the airports stricter. When I walked into that tunnel and onto the airplane, I was relieved beyond belief.

The flight was half-full. Nobody wanted to fly to the US. I could have sat almost anywhere. I stayed in my original seat and slept most of the time, listening to the airplane-piped music. I ate, I drank. And I did worry a bit as well. But I knew I was going home, and that made me happy.

The airplane touched down at Houston on time. Everyone gathered their carry-on bags and headed for immigration. I waited for a few minutes, as the lines for US citizens were somewhat long. After re-entering US soil I almost broke down. Even though I was still almost three thousand miles away from my final destination, I was in The United States. I collected my luggage and called a local hotel for a room. Then I waited in the warm Houston sun for the express to pick me up. When I exited the airport, the place was swarming with police. I talked briefly with one of them and she told me it was because of the attacks and the beefing up of the security at the airports. Then my express came to pick me up and take me to the hotel.

It was a Days Inn. It was behind a mall, and next to a water tank. The air conditioning was blasting away in the lobby as I signed in for my room. I took the elevator to the third floor and found my room. I dumped my bags next to the bed and went out to buy a soft drink at the vending machine. I also got some ice from the ice machine. Then I called my mom at work. She was happy that I had arrived safely to Houston. She told me that she had talked to my aunt and that she wouldn't be able to pick me up at the airport, so I would have to take a cab home. I understood. It was good to talk to my mom. We talked for about fifteen minutes, and then she had to go. I told her I would call her when I got to Hawaii.

241

I spent all of my time watching television. For the first three weeks, I hadn't watched a second of television. Then in the last three days I had almost made up for that. I watched all of the events unfolding in the aftermath of the terrorist attacks. I actually had this sense of foreboding. Whether it was because of the attacks or something from myself, I couldn't put my finger on it. I ate half a cookie, set the alarm for six, and then had a restless night of waking up and sleeping.

Day 24

I again awoke earlier than the alarm. Five-thirty and dark outside. The television was still on and I had left a light on. I re-packed my backpack, changed clothes, and put on my shoes. The wake-up call came at six. I went down to the lobby at six-thirty. There were actually a few people there. I waited until the express came to take me to the airport. When I went into the departures area, there were quite a few people there. I guess there were a lot of people traveling, and that took me by surprise, knowing that not too many people were flying because of the terrorist attacks and the hijacking of the airplanes. I checked in and then there was a new procedure I was introduced to. After checking in, they examined my luggage. A couple of people took my bags, put them on a shiny metal table, and proceeded to rub a dark, circular cloth inside them. These clothes, I was told, swept up any particles into them. Afterwards, the cloths would be put into a machine that could detect anything from explosives to drugs. I was negative on both and my luggage was placed on the conveyor belt to be loaded onto the airplane.

I walked through the metal detector and x-ray machine, and then walked to the gate. I sat at my departure gate for an hour and a half listening to a relaxation tape with my eyes closed. It always seemed that if I closed my eyes the time would go faster. Then I heard the loudspeaker, and the female voice announced that my flight would be boarding. I walked to the gate entrance, handed my ticket to the flight attendant, and then walked down the sloping tunnel that led to the airplane opening. A smiling attendant ushered me in, and I sat down at my aisle seat. I sighed deeply and relaxed. I was on the final part of my journey home, and I let a little stress out. Seven more hours and I would be back where I started three and a half weeks ago.

The flight went fast. I was seated next to a young woman who was in the Army. She was an army nurse at a military hospital. The airplane was actually going onward to Guam. That was where she was headed. She had the strongest Northeastern accent I ever heard. Most of the time I listened to the airplane music and slept. And when I was awake I ate and drank. I kept to myself mostly. The airplane touched down at Honolulu International Airport at 12:35 PM local time, and as the wheels screeched on the tarmac, I let all the stress go. I had made it back safely. But I did feel a little sad and frustrated. Sad, because I would miss Terri and that I wasn't able to complete my journey. Frustrated, because I felt that I was not prepared and that it wasn't just myself that contributed to my failure in completing my trip. As I left the airplane, the traditional hot, humid air didn't hit me. It was a mild, almost chilled air. I walked across the bridge that connected the gates to the main airport. It felt strange. People were walking around like zombies, and the atmosphere was subdued. Without speaking one word, I picked up my bags, and got a cab to take me back to my grandma's house.

I paid the cab driver well for the trip. Then I walked up to the house and went in through the back. Sunny, my grandma's golden retriever, started barking up a storm. I went in the back door and scared the heck out of the dog. She was always happy to see me before, but I must have spooked her good because she cowered away from me. My grandma came to the window and said hi. I coaxed Sunny into letting me pet her. Then she must have remembered my scent because her tail started swishing violently back and forth, and she jumped up on her hind legs and put her paws on my shoulders. I was attacked with a barrage of licks on my face. I put her down and kissed her big black nose. Then I went in the house and wearily dropped my bags on the redwood floor. I was home…

Epilogue- for now

I have been here for five days. I have started a new journal for my new life here in Hawaii. But there isn't a day that goes by (only five, mind you, so far) that I'm not wondering if my trip would have turned out fine if I had stayed. When I wake up early in the morning, I feel a sense of loneliness and emptiness. I miss being on the road, waking up in a foreign country, in a foreign city. A new culture living and breathing right outside of your room, and all you have to do is start walking on the streets and you are right in the thick of it. The new sights, smells, sounds, tastes and people that will invariably be a part of you forever. I am in a place that I have known all my life. Not that I am unthankful or ungrateful for being here. Hawaii is one of the most beautiful places I have ever been to, and even more, it holds some of the most important, touching memories of my life. Perhaps it wasn't quite my time to go on my journey. Maybe I wasn't ready. I might never be ready. But I believe that my spirit still wants to wander the world and learn. I hope that someday I will get a chance to do that again.

About The Author

Steve Baba is a poet and writer. He teaches poetry workshops around the country. He calls NYC, Santa Fe, Honolulu and San Francisco as his homes. Currently working on a memoir, Steve lives in San Francisco.